looking for
redfeather

This is a work of fiction. Many of the places are real, but the characters and the incidents are products of the author's imagination. Any similarity to persons living or dead is entirely coincidental — except for Geronimo, Cochise, Victorio, and Lozen, who were very real.

Fiction House, Ltd.
Steamboat Springs, Colorado.
Copyright © 2013 Linda Collison
All rights reserved.
ISBN: 0989365301
ISBN 13 trade paperback: 978-0-9893653-0-7
ISBN13 electronic edition: 978-0-9893653-1-4
Library of Congress Control Number: 2013945962
Fiction House Ltd, Steamboat Springs, CO

Cover design by Albert Roberts

Also by Linda Collison

Novels

Barbados Bound
Surgeon's Mate
Star-Crossed

Non-fiction

Rocky Mountain Wineries; a travel guide to the wayside vineyards
(with Bob Russell)
Colorado Kids; a statewide family outdoor adventure guide
(with Bob Russell)

Looking for Redfeather

by

Linda Collison

Fiction House, Ltd.
Steamboat Springs, Colorado

"We are the children of one God. The sun, the darkness, the winds
are all listening to what we have to say."

– Goyathlay (Geronimo)

1

Ramie left Cheyenne in a hailstorm, tramping up the on-ramp to Interstate 25, right past the NO HITCHHIKING sign, his thumb in the air. A raging purple sky hurled hailstones and forks of lightning at him, but the boy pulled his hat down and kept on walking.

A driving guitar rhythm from the off-brand mp3 player in his pocket filled his head. The thunder of Audioslave matched the wrathful weather and infused him with energy and purpose, propelling his feet forward, lifting his thumb even as it lifted his heart. Hitchhiking was like knocking at a door: it felt hopeful—like a question (Going my way?) somehow more potent than lifting the middle finger, a digit he was more familiar with using. *Fuck you* had become a feeble cliché, a cheap shot in the dark.

Just as suddenly as it had come on, the storm was over, leaving the air scrubbed clean, smelling of wet dirt and sage. The sun reappeared like nothing had happened and a southbound semi roared by, throwing a rainbow of slush from its wheels. Ramie shivered, his wet shirt clinging to his back. Tumbleweeds skipped across the highway, piling up against a barbed wire fence. A shredded Walmart bag caught on a roadside thistle. *How I feel*, he thought. Hailstones melting, crunching underfoot. His new shoes burned blisters on his feet with every step.

Blue skies now, and fresh-washed chicory. To the west, the Medicine Bow Mountains were stark cutouts on the horizon. But Ramie was headed south. Redfeather—had he been in Denver all along? Then again, the name could be a coincidence. Didn't matter. School was out, and Cheyenne had become too small to contain him.

Though he had often imagined his exodus, when it came right down to it, Ramie had left on a whim. So many times he had searched for Redfeather on the library's computer. Redfeather—Raymond Redfeather—his own name, but it wasn't himself he was looking for. This time he had come up with a lead, just a hundred miles south in Denver, Colorado, a place he had never been. That had been the clincher. Ramie had stuffed a change of clothes in his pack, scribbled a few words to his mother on the back of a past-due notice, grabbed a fistful of bills from her tip jar, and lit out for the highway.

His recklessness warmed and expanded him. Cornell's voice and Morello's guitar riffs drove him, encouraged him, comforted him, gave rhythm to his step, and filled his skull with *sound*. Inside his head, still largely unexplored, he spun through the universe like some unnamed comet, a meteorite, or an asteroid yet to be discovered.

A car passed him. The brake lights flashed red, a squeal of tires and a spray of gravel as it veered to a stop on the shoulder of the highway, fifty yards ahead. It was a big land yacht, an old Cadillac Eldorado, the rear chrome bumper and the Maryland antique license plate splattered with mud. *Who sees Maryland license plates out here?* Even though there was an air force base in Cheyenne with airmen and officers from all over the country, Ramie couldn't recall ever seeing Maryland tags on a vehicle. *And where is Maryland, anyhow? Somewhere between Rhode Island and Virginia, or maybe next to Ohio?* He remembered the puzzle his mother had gotten him from the thrift store years ago; it had been missing a state. He was pretty sure it was Maryland that had been lost.

How weird that he should catch a ride in this collector's car, a rich old man's car, a ride from the past, a cream colored Cadillac covered with mud and road tar. His breath came in gulps; he tried to gain control of it as he slouched his way toward the vehicle. Like he was in no particular rush. He almost changed his mind, but something drove him on. Approaching the car, he reached into his pocket and silenced the music.

The driver lowered the passenger window and grinned across the expansive seat. It was a young face, a face that hadn't seen much sun. Wraparound shades obscured his eyes. He was wearing a black felt cowboy hat that screamed *poseur*.

"Hey, bro, where you headed?" the driver said.

Ramie sized him up. He wasn't very big. Unless he had a gun, Ramie felt sure he could handle him. If it came to that.

"Denver," Ramie said with a slight shrug. Like, whatever. He wasn't begging, he wasn't desperate. Give me a ride or not, I don't really care. He maintained his punk face, as his mother called it, lowering his eyelids lazily and pulling the corner of his shapely bottom lip into a don't-give-a-shit sneer that said, *Go on, fuck with me. I dare you.* But his fingertips tingled and his heart made itself known to him, shaking the bars of its cage.

"Ha! Denver? What serendipity! Hop in." The driver, no more than a teenager himself, swept a mound of ketchup-stained fast-food wrappers and empty Red Bull cans from the passenger's side of the front seat onto the floor.

"Don't mind the mess, I've been on the road for, like, twenty hours straight. Glad you came along; I was getting bored. Hey, you got caught in that hailstorm, didn't you? That was freaking awesome! Like being shot at, like being strafed. Insanely loud on the roof of the car, I'm talking incredible." The driver showered him with a flood of words and a wave of exuberance nearly as torrential as the cloudburst had been.

"Yeah. Uh, sorry, I'm a little wet," Ramie said. Water dripped from the bill of his backward cap, trickling down his neck.

The young driver grinned. "No problem-o. Won't hurt those leather seats; they're bulletproof. Throw your shit in the back and hop in!"

Ramie had never ridden in a Cadillac. He felt like he was in a movie, like he was getting into a limousine, or maybe a time machine. He put his guitar in the back as instructed then slid onto the big, wide seat, like a leather couch. No seat belts, even. The smells of cigarette smoke and cold french fries were thick in the air. He took off his cap and ran his hand through his wild shock of hair. Glanced in the rearview mirror at his reflection, which always startled him. *Can that be me?*

Who would have thought it would be so damn easy? The highway had been there his whole life, just waiting for him to pack his shit and go stand on the ramp, stick his thumb in the breeze, and catch the first carpet ride out of town.

2

The girl called Faith Appleby was no more. Faith was dead; long live Mae B. LaRoux! Mae B. *May be.* It was a hopeful name, filled with possibilities, and, most importantly, it was a name she had chosen herself. The driver's license in her pocket was a good fake, but expensive. It had cost her fifty bucks—taken dollar by dollar from the church collection plate.

The girl toyed with the new silver stud in her tongue, tapping it against her teeth as she looked out the bus window. Kansas had been endless, miles and miles and miles of green and brown fields, and when they'd finally crossed the line into Colorado, she had wondered where the mountains were. Wasn't Colorado where people went skiing? Where were the mountains? she had wondered as the bus rolled across Colorado's eastern plains. The sign had said WELCOME TO COLORFUL COLORADO, but it still looked like Kansas. Green and brown; green and brown. Oh, but a praise-God blue sky overhead. Finally, two hours later, she saw them—the mountains—far away on the horizon, a jagged purple majesty *above the fruited plain. America, America, God shed his grace on thee. And crown thy good with brotherhood, from sea to shining sea,* she sang the words in her head.

Route 40 became East Colfax Avenue, running through a scattering of tumbledown buildings that seemed to have sprung up out of the plains. It was all rather tattered looking. Seedy, her mother would call it. But seeds held promise. The bus sped on past empty parking lots with weeds growing in the cracks of the asphalt, peeling billboards covered with graffiti, clusters of falling-down buildings and busted-out neon signs like a trail of broken dreams. She looked at the ruin with detachment, knowing she would succeed where others had failed.

Mae B. LaRoux. The sound of the name enthralled her. Everybody should get to choose his or her own name; it should be some sort of coming-of-age ceremony, like confirmation or a Mexican—what was the word? *Quinceañera?* Name-choosing should involve white dresses, a party, and gifts. Lots of gifts.

A green sign outside the bus window announced AURORA, which made her think of *aurora borealis,* but she couldn't remember what those words meant. Something in the heavens, a constellation? Maybe. Mae B. Aurora would be a pretty name for a girl. Maybe she should change her name to Aurora after this Colorado town that continued to unfold like a moving picture outside the window. Nail salons, Mexican restaurants, pawn shops, Big-O Tires, dollar stores—oh, look, a cluster of people waiting at a bus stop. Some were texting and some were smoking and some looked wistfully at the Greyhound as it rolled on by. Like they wished they were on it, following their dreams. What did they dream of?

She shrugged her shoulders to relieve the kink in her neck, a result of keeping her head turned sideways—which wasn't only to look out the window but also to avoid any eye contact with the man sitting next to her. She could feel his roving eyes. He smelled bad and he talked a lot, though she wasn't sure if he was talking to her or to someone else. Maybe he was talking to his guardian angel.

Three days ago the former Faith Appleby had left Baton Rouge on a Greyhound bus for Kansas City, hoping to pick up a few gigs before continuing on to Austin where the music festival would be held. Luke, her older brother, lived in Austin—he was going to college there—and she planned to sleep on his sofa.

But Faith, now Mae B., had not gotten any gigs in Kansas City. All she had found there was her first tattoo and a tongue piercing, a twofer special at KC Ink. Running low on money, she had gotten on the bus. The wrong bus, as it turned out. Mae B. thought she had bought a ticket to Austin, but somehow she ended up on the bus to Denver. Her geography wasn't that good to begin with, and the signs at the Greyhound station in Kansas City had been so confusing—they kept changing every few minutes—and the disembodied announcements over the loudspeaker sounded like God's voice, authoritative but unintelligible.

Her mistake didn't trouble her much; she trusted luck and her guardian angel. Maybe there was a reason for Denver. The tattoo artist had spoken well of it as he'd pricked her skin and infused it with lurid color. He had spent some time in D-town, as he called it, and had talked about some of the blues bars there: Ziggies, Bushwhackers, Herb's Hideaway. She recalled those names and was thrilled by the sound of them. The sound of words, the way they felt coming out of your mouth, was important. Words were powerful: they could cast spells, make people angry, or reduce them to tears. Some words could be made into names and completely transform you. For example, Ziggie LaRoux. Hmmm. Had she been too quick to choose the name Mae B.? Maybe she should just go by LaRoux. LaRoux could be her permanent name, and she could change her first name from time to time. She thought about how women changed their last names when they got married. She would be LaRoux forever and change her first name to suit the situation.

Her parents would be horrified if they knew where she really was, what she was doing. They would be aghast. *A ghast. A ghost.* Seeing a ghost would make somebody aghast, it would make them *gasp*. She was pleased at the way the words connected in her mind, and pleased because her parents had been so easily fooled. LaRoux had told them she and Jordan Merriweather were going to be counselors at the Ozark Bible Camp, a good alibi since she and Jordan (the golden girl, the approved friend) had attended the camp since they were eight years old. She had given Jordan her cell phone, with its GPS tracking device, and instructed her friend to text the mother daily, and to sign off with PTL and KTF, which was family code for *Praise the Lord* and *Keep the Faith*, a play on the name LaRoux had been christened with.

LaRoux had left Faith behind. Left her for dead, and she was as good as buried, that miserable creature raised in captivity and cruelly misused. Having discovered her one God-given gift, LaRoux knew she must leave home before her parents managed to destroy it. Her voice— a secret gift, a rich vein of pure silver. A force of nature, a phenomenon that had recently found its pleasure in the blues, a genre of music she had discovered via her Uncle Jim, who wasn't an uncle by blood but her father's stepbrother. He had taught her to play chords on a three-quarter-size guitar he'd given her when she was eight. Uncle Jim didn't come around anymore, but she could watch his videos on YouTube. Blues wasn't very popular among other kids her age, but Faith Appleby, so recently reborn as Mae B. LaRoux, was convinced she was from another time and place, because she certainly didn't fit well in this world.

Her parents did not like blues music; it was not a welcome sound in the Appleby household. "Can't you at least find a Christian rock station?" Her parents had no music in their souls, and she wondered if maybe Uncle Jim was her real father. Thank God for earbuds; she could listen to anything she liked. The world inside her head was her own, she had discovered.

Music was everywhere. Music was in the blood and bones of Baton Rouge, her hometown. When LaRoux began to discover the music within, it had been electrifying. *I can do something! I have a gift!* But the parents were suspicious. *Where did you get that guitar, and who taught you to play it? Uncle Jim gave it to me; he taught me to play it, don't you remember? We don't talk about Uncle Jim anymore, and he isn't really your uncle anyway.*

She never knew what happened to Uncle Jim. Her parents never would say. When she asked, they responded with cryptic sentences that were not explanations at all, but riddles. They warned her about the dangers that come from thinking impure thoughts and listening to licentious music. *Licentious. Lie-sin-shus.* Yet the blues wasn't lies or sins, the blues was truths put to words and sung to chords. The blues was wounds exposed to air, wounds that scabbed over but never really healed. Jesus knew about the blues, and his words, when sung to blues chords, made her tremble, they were so true-blue. It must be her parents who were lying. She had suspected it for some time.

LaRoux didn't consider herself a runaway, not at sixteen. Her friend Jordan had told her that in some states girls could legally marry at sixteen; they could become emancipated. She might be considered a missing person, except she wasn't yet missing. If she got noticed at the New Blues Festival in Austin, won the Break Out Blues competition and landed a contract, she'd tell the parents the truth, and they'd just have to deal with it. Maybe she should get emancipated, but she wasn't sure how to go about it or what exactly it meant. Was it some sort of document, like a driver's license? Did it mean you didn't have to live with, or obey, your parents anymore? She hoped it didn't require any math, because numbers weren't her thing. They held no meaning for her.

Then again, maybe her parents would be relieved she was gone. Maybe they weren't even her real parents. *May be.*

The man next to her raised his voice. He was becoming quite excited; it made her nervous. She looked around for an empty seat, but the only other place was in the very back, next to a slack-jawed sleeping man who managed to take up both seats in his sprawl. Most of the passengers were men. Just a few women travelers, older women who had somehow managed to sit together, some prearrangement, some secret girl talk that eluded LaRoux.

The world outside her home was a foreign land, and she wasn't fluent in the language. Her parents had tried to protect her from a dangerous and dirty society, but she was a cat slipping out the back door and leaping nimbly over the fence. Gone.

Dr. Sanders had said learning difficulties were to be expected, part of the genetic syndrome. He called it a microdeletion on the q arm of the twenty-second chromosome—22q deletion syndrome. LaRoux didn't like having a syndrome, but she liked the catchy way 22 and Q rhymed. They were referred to a genetic counselor who told them there was no cure, but that she would benefit from further testing and specialized instruction in a supportive environment for children with learning differences. But her parents didn't want to hear it. They didn't believe in syndromes or genetics, just like they didn't believe in evolution and global warming. God's will—that's what they believed in. *Thy will be done* was their answer to everything. Though, apparently, God's will could only be revealed through the Bible, ordained ministers, and certain politicians, certainly not through the voice of a genetic counselor— or a sixteen-year-old girl whom Satan surely flirted with and tempted.

LaRoux turned up the volume on her music player, KT Tunstall's voice and energetic guitar strumming now filling her head, drowning out the ranting from the man sitting next to her.

There is a reason for everything; everything that happened, happened for a reason. She believed this, fully. It was her version of *Thy will be done.* Getting on the wrong bus was a mistake that was meant to happen. Coming to Denver was surely meant to be an opening act to next month's music festival in Austin and its Break Out Blues Contest, where she would be discovered. Sometimes mistakes can lead to something better, something fine. LaRoux's skin sensed impending fortune with a tingling that spread from her scalp to her fingertips. Rafael, her guardian angel (flamboyantly dressed and quite possibly gay), gave her a thumbs-up from outside the bus where he flew along at seventy miles an hour, keeping up effortlessly, as only an angel can do. *I got your back, babe.*

The strange man next to her sniffed and snorted, gathering mucous from the depths of his gorge like he was sucking up the last of a milkshake. LaRoux hunkered against the window, turning up the volume of her iPod to the max. Now it was Gwen Stefani singing a sassy tune about a cheerleader who wasn't gonna take no smack. She liked that attitude.

LaRoux's musical tastes weren't limited to the blues; she liked to listen to all sorts of musical styles. She particularly liked the alternative rock of Evanescence and a little-known Goth band she had heard in Kansas City called Decaying Kiss. But whenever she opened her throat to sing, blues is what came out from deep inside her body. The different kinds of music—blues, hip-hop, country, classical—were like flowers in a sound garden. *Soundgarden!* Pleased with this wordplay (she searched her brain for the word *metaphor* but couldn't find it), she pressed her nose against the window and watched East Colfax Avenue slide by as Soundgarden's lyrics bloomed in her head.

"Next stop, Denver terminal," the driver announced over a scratchy loudspeaker system. LaRoux had never been to Denver, and she knew no one there. The word brought nothing to mind except the Broncos and Denver omelets, yet she liked the sound of the name. If she ever had a boy baby or a dog, she'd name him Denver.

Tall buildings on either side, the bus had entered the heart of the city. Passengers started gathering their belongings, preparing to get off. There was something in the air, a sense of excitement or possibility. She would have herself a look around town, try to pick up some gigs at the blues bars, and if she made some money, she would get a new tattoo as a souvenir. There would be plenty of time for Austin. She could take a bus to Austin from Denver whenever she wanted—buses go everywhere— if she could just make a little money here, enough to tide her over.

3

Charles Sweeney (who had quite recently dumped the unfortunate nickname Chuck and assumed the moniker Chas) was driving a stolen Cadillac along Lincoln Avenue in Cheyenne, marveling at a stray tumbleweed rolling down the road in front of him. After sixteen hundred miles, he had finally reached the Real Deal. Wyoming was the West he had imagined: sagebrush, prairie dogs, antelope, and overhead an ocean of sky. Cheyenne was a sprawling settlement, a rough-and-ready town named for an Indian tribe. A frontier town. Across the dun-colored buttes, he could see pointed mountains, like teepees on the horizon.

But Chas was lonely, having lost his traveling companion back in Chicago. All of his friends had backed out except Patrick—and Patrick had gotten homesick after only two days on the road. He'd come up with some lame excuse, but basically Patrick had experienced a crisis of confidence. He had chickened out, the little puss, and Chas had to drive him to O'Hare International Airport and hold his hand while he waited on standby to fly back to Baltimore. Back to Mommy and Daddy and a summer job, back to his Aunt Nancy's Fourth of July backyard barbecue, back to a life so boring and predictable it nearly put Chas Sweeney into a fit of narcolepsy imagining it.

Wyoming could've been fun if Patrick had stayed. Chas needed somebody to talk to, to share the experience with. Like, look at those antelope! Right there alongside the road, practically inside the city limits, staring at him with curiosity. Who knew? There were more antelope than people in this state, he had read that somewhere.

Chas was a voracious reader, an absorber of random facts, a walking Wikipedia. What he didn't know, he invented. For someone who, until last week, had never been further away from home than Ocean City, Maryland (well, except for the one excursion to Disney World when he was five—too young for it to count because he didn't remember it), Chas Sweeney carried an atlas in his head. He had a mind for such things. Place names stuck to his brain. Geography was his strong suit. He liked to read, and he was good with maps. Capital cities and interstate highways were engraved in the deepening grooves of his cerebral cortex. "If you'd apply yourself in school, you'd be formidable," Gran often said.

Kid Rock did his Detroit rap number, the one about being a West Coast cowboy pimp in a convertible.

Actually, the car was not stolen, just borrowed (without asking). Chas had thought it better to beg forgiveness than to ask permission— and there was no way in hell his grandmother would ever give him permission to drive this car, a pristine champagne-colored 1960 Cadillac Eldorado. Gran had inherited the classic ride from George, her third husband, recently deceased. Old George had kept his baby in mint condition for forty-one years, hermetically sealed in a custom-made cover inside a climate-controlled garage. The car was a shrine, a sacred object the old coot had worshipped. The odometer had read 9,999 miles when Chas had backed it out of the garage. It had read that for decades; it would be sacrilege to go beyond four digits—it would decrease its value by hundreds, if not thousands, of dollars.

But what good was a car just sitting in the garage? Gran never drove it—she had her Lexus—and Chas didn't think he was in line to inherit it when she passed on. If he knew his grandmother, she would probably bequeath the car to further Alzheimer's research. Her late husband had suffered from that form of dementia. Chas and Gran had witnessed the slow, gradual decline of George's mind until he no longer recognized them and could not be trusted alone in the house. He became restless, agitated, and incapable of reason. He hit Gran, knocked her down, and had to be put in a home. It was a nice place, as far as nursing homes go, but George was a wanderer, and one night he escaped. The old man just lit out. He took off walking (toward his real home, uncannily enough), and when he tried to cross the street against the light, he was struck by a truck and killed.

Gran had nearly collapsed with anguish, but Chas thought it was a rather heroic ending. The way the old man died trying to come home. Kind of like a dark version of Ulysses. You never know when your number will be up; you never know for sure when you're going to die, or how. Chas could not even imagine himself as an old man. He was sure he would die young.

But it wasn't dying that he wanted to think about, it was living. He wanted to live—really live, as in the verb *to live*—not just exist. So he had taken the sacred keys and split, leaving a note. A long note. An essay, actually, a wordy treatise defending himself. He knew Gran would shit a brick when she read it, but by then he'd be halfway through Ohio, and what could she do then? He had pulled over at a rest stop outside of Columbus to listen to her panicked voice mails and call her back with a calm, somewhat contrite reply. But he was not coming home, not yet. Chas convinced her he was going on a college tour, this being the summer before his senior year, the summer when all the other college-bound kids were visiting universities, interviewing, and filling out college applications.

Gran wanted him to go to college, although her hopes for an Ivy League school had been dashed when, in the ninth grade, Chas had been suspended for smoking weed in the boys' room. Though he had been grounded for half the year, she hadn't given up on him. "You will go to college and make something of yourself, Charles," she had said over and over. *Unlike your mother or your father* was left unspoken.

Gran wanted him to become an astrophysicist or an architect. Or an attorney. Attorneys sometimes went on to become senators and presidents. She would settle for him being an archaeologist. Chas thought if he was limited to careers that began with A, he'd choose to be a famous actor or author—but his guardian dismissed both of those choices.

"You give me no choice but to call the police; I'm at my wits' end. Your grandfather would roll over in his grave," Gran scolded him over the phone. "He worshipped that car."

He wasn't my grandfather, Chas thought. *The old grump never said more than two words to me. Besides, the man is dead, and it's a waste to keep a useful thing like a car in a garage and never drive it.*

"But Gran, I need it more than he does right now. There aren't any parking lots in heaven."

He hoped he had made her smile with that wisecrack. Probably not, but maybe just a little. She could be a mean old woman, but she had a good sense of humor. A sharp mind.

"You might have asked me. This is nonsense."

"Don't call the cops, Gran. Please. You know I'm not a thief. I'll bring the car back after I've toured the campuses. "

"I have called your father and told him about your latest escapade."

Oh, like he cares. Chas had heard nothing from Charles the Elder, neither did he expect to. His father was living in a halfway house and wearing an ankle bracelet for multiple DUIs and possession of various illegal substances. His father had his own troubles. Marrying Gran's daughter had been the one fine thing Charles Sweeney Sr. had done in his life. But the marriage had ended by the time little Chuckie was in kindergarten. His father was a loser, it pained him to admit. And his mother—well, that was another story altogether, and he didn't want to think about her right now.

"Sorry, Gran, you're breaking up. Sorry, what? I don't have much of a signal. Losing you. Call you soon." He shut off the phone. The mention of his father had ruined his exuberance.

Chas's family was broken—shattered—they were one continual, slow-motion collision, a sixteen-car pileup on the highway, a recurring, never-ending accident. He'd had to leave the scene; he'd had to take a detour. He'd had to get the hell out of Maryland before he too was pronounced brain-dead. All of his friends were fuckups too; they were blind, deaf, and lame, stuck back there in the sweltering East Coast summer (*It's the heat; no, it's the humidity*), working their boring, dead-end, minimum-wage summer jobs. Only he had the good sense to break free, to take old dead George's car and flee the scene. Now he was sixteen hundred miles away, flying down the highway, cruising across the southeastern edge of Wyoming (Wyoming! Wide open spaces! Bucking cowboys on the license plates, fucking tumbleweeds rolling down the road!) looking for his real life.

But without somebody to discover it with him, the world was a harsh, inhospitable place. Hail battered the windshield like bullets. He and Patrick had talked about hiking Yellowstone and climbing the Grand Tetons. They had talked about camping out on the Wind River Indian Reservation, sleeping under the stars before pressing on to California, to San Francisco, the Pacific Coast Highway, Malibu. Or maybe Seattle, instead. But none of that had come to pass, because Patrick had given up. Chas might as well blow this town and head south, for Denver.

Chas turned his phone back on and took a video out the window to post on Facebook and Twitter. This was Cheyenne on a June afternoon, 2008. Railroad tracks, oil refineries, drive-through liquor stores, and budget motels. He pulled off the road into an Arby's parking lot to text Patrick. *Check this out ImaY O Ming mfukr! u?*

Actually, he didn't care where Patrick was; he already knew. Mowing his parents' lawn. Or slapping meat and cheese at Subway. Or possibly slapping meat to his sister's Victoria Secret catalogs in his cool, dark bedroom, landscaped with hills of dirty laundry. That's why they had taken off, wasn't it? To get away from that routine, that crushing boredom, to see the planet before it was obliterated by a meteor or suffocated on its own exhaust. Two days out Patrick, the little puss, had gotten scared, gotten homesick, started whining about going home. To what?

Chas had a need to talk. To communicate. He had more to say than he could possibly text, way more to say than his friends cared to read on their tiny, greasy-finger-smudged screens. He wanted to express what he was seeing—that the sky out here was incomprehensibly huge and aloof, the deer and the antelope really did play, the raptors ruled from their perches on top of electric poles. And the men drove pickups with mud flaps and gun racks. They wore hats and boots. Chas had bought himself a twenty-dollar cowboy hat at a truck stop on Lincoln Avenue. Cheap. But at a distance, it could pass for a Stetson or a Resistol. He held the iPhone at arm's length and took a couple of shots of himself behind the wheel, cigarette hanging out of his mouth. *Yeah, I'm a cowboy, bee-atch!*

Words spun inside his head, picking up more words like dust in a maelstrom. He dreamed in monologues, woke up talking, had written whole novels in his head. He had begun to talk at eighteen months, and when other toddlers were saying their first words, Chas was conversing in sentences, using prepositional phrases with ease. He had the gift of gab and did much to contribute to the wealth of words bouncing around the universe. Chas bragged, boasted, joked, cajoled, boasted, wheedled, questioned, explained, ranted, quipped, lambasted, and complained. He was good at it; he was amazing when it came to run-on sentences, emphatic statements, exclamations, and exhortations. But now Chas was alone, and his words seemed to bounce around inside the car like so many hollow ping-pong balls.

Glancing at himself in the rearview mirror, he squeezed a pimple on his chin single-handedly. Bared his teeth for inspection. He could have been halfway decent-looking if his teeth were straighter, but there had been more pressing problems during those formative years. Chas didn't want braces now; he was too old for braces. People would think he was thirteen. He was working on a way of smiling that didn't show his teeth. Working on his sense of humor, honing it fine, so that people wouldn't notice his crooked teeth. His lack of height. His little comma of a penis.

Chas dialed in a new playlist, Classic Road Songs, dialed up the volume, and Tom Petty's ballad about chasing a dream blared out of the speakers. Chas checked the GPS—Denver, one hundred miles south. The city called him; it was a gigantic electromagnet, a tractor beam, and he was hurtling toward the city on a collision course. In Denver there would be people to talk to, people to receive his random thoughts and observations. There would be events, concerts, any number of thrilling encounters. He would hurl himself into the rush of humanity.

Accelerating up the on-ramp to I-25, tires squealing, Chas felt a rush of excitement. Then, seeing the hitchhiker, he impulsively braked, pulling over on the shoulder in a shower of stones. That's when he noticed the hail damage, the pock marks all over the hood of the Cadillac. He fought to keep his heart from sinking. *She's going to kill me.* Then again, Gran didn't see very well. And with everything else on her mind, the train wreck in slow-mo that was their collective life, maybe she wouldn't even notice.

4

"You smoke?" Chas held out a pack of Marlboros.

Ramie didn't smoke, but he took one anyway. He didn't want to seem superior or judgmental.

Chas handed him the lighter. "Name's Chas. You?"

Ramie didn't answer right away. He fumbled to light his cigarette, stalling for time.

"I mean, if you don't want to tell me, no problem. Or give me an alias; that works."

"Ramie."

"Hey, Ramie." They bumped fists.

Chas cracked the wing and blew smoke out the side of his mouth as he accelerated into the left lane, the speedometer creeping up toward ninety.

"Gotta love the speed limit out here. Back home, it's like fifty-five. So lame-o." Impulsively, he belted out the classic line in good Sammy Hagar fashion. "I can't drive no fifty-five!"

Ramie smiled to cover his nervousness.

"I'm from Reisterstown," said Chas. "Ever heard of it?"

Ramie shook his head.

"Don't worry, you're not alone. Nobody's heard of Reisterstown. It's like a suburb of Baltimore. You've heard of Baltimore, haven't you?"

Ramie nodded. "Ravens. Orioles."

"Hell, yeah! And don't forget the Terrapins. You like basketball? And we got lacrosse, Johns Hopkins University, the USS *Constellation*, Fort McHenry, Edgar Allen Poe's grave—all in Baltimore. Yeah, I'm a Balti-moron by association. I was born in Baltimore, at GBMC. In Towson. Which is another suburb of Baltimore. I fucking hate the suburbs."

Ramie nodded, drawing on the cigarette. He was glad for it now; it gave him something to do. It made him feel disconnected.

"Ever been there? To Baltimore?"

Ramie shook his head. The cigarette was building up quite an ash, and he wasn't sure what he should do with it. The ashtray was overflowing. He couldn't see the window controls. The ash fell into his lap.

"Ha! Don't bother. You ain't missing shit; they're all brain-dead back there. That's why I got the hell out. I'm on the road, looking for sentient life in the universe. Hey, Ramie, you from Cheyenne? I mean, do you live there, or were you just passing through?"

"I live there."

"Sweet. Cheyenne is badass. Wish I was from there."

"No, you don't."

"Are you kidding me? I'd trade you places any day."

Reisterstown must be the pits, Ramie thought.

"Why is it, bro?" Chas continued. "Why are there no trees? Did a meteor strike wipe out all of your trees? There's been, like, no trees in the last four states I've been through. Ever since I left Chicago, the world has been, like, devoid of trees."

"What do you mean? There are trees."

"Ha! Where? Where are the trees?" Chas gestured at the broad expanse of rolling plain surrounding them.

Ramie shrugged. "They're around. You just have to know where to look."

"What are they, miniature trees? One inch high? Lilliputian shrubs? I'm talking about actual, full-size trees. Big oaks and shit. Not that I'm complaining, 'cause out here what you got is a lot of sky. Back east we have trees but not much sky. The sky back where I come from is, like, nondescript. All thick and hazy and murky, no color at all. Well, except in October and January. That's when you get your crisp, blue sky. Most of the time, you never give it much thought. Most of the time. Sometimes it gets to you, like when it's gray skies and rain for two weeks on end, then you want to go blow your brains out, but you don't have a gun. Or you have a gun but no bullets. And besides, maybe this is the last day of blah; maybe tomorrow the sun is going to bust out, and you don't want to miss that. Ha! But trees we got. Lots and lots of trees. You can get lost in the fuckers, and people find bodies in the woods, back home. In various states of decay, I might add."

"Out here we don't have woods. We have forests."

"Oh, excuse me. Forests. What are they, miniature forests? Just kidding, dude, I love it out here."

"The forests are in the mountains. Up there." Ramie jerked his head to the right where a low line of purple mountains rimmed the horizon. "The Rocky Mountains."

"Shit! The mountains, the fucking Rocky Mountains! I can't believe I'm here. You ever climb a mountain, Ramie? You ever climb one of those fuckers? I would love to climb a mountain. Actually, I'd like to shred one on a board. You ride?"

Ramie shrugged. "I skateboard. A little." Actually, he had given his skateboard to his younger brother; he had never mastered it. He had never mastered anything. Besides, snowboarding was a sport for rich kids. Lift tickets cost a fortune. "There's a cottonwood," he said, lifting his cigarette. "A grove of them."

"A cottonwood?"

"A cottonwood tree. You said you wanted to see a tree."

"Shit, I missed it." Chas looked in the rearview mirror, but he didn't see the cottonwoods. "You're the first hitchhiker I've ever picked up, you know? My first hitchhiker ever. Tell me you're not a psycho, a Columbine wannabe. A deranged kid with a Glock in your backpack. Good thing you're not wearing a trench coat."

Ramie had to laugh; it just burst out of him. "Funny, I was wondering the same thing about you. Hoping you weren't a criminal or pervert or something."

"Well, I am something, and I might be a criminal, but I'm not dangerous. Now that we've cleared the air on that, where are we going, Ramie?"

"Denver. That's where I'm headed."

"Duh. Denver is big. It's got a population of 2.7 million, so could you be a little more specific?"

"I'm going to Ziggies."

"Ziggies?"

"Ziggies."

"What's Ziggies?"

"A bar."

"Cool. Why are we going there?"

"We? I don't know about you, but I'm looking for Redfeather."

"Who's Redfeather?"

"My father. I think." Ramie's gut twisted apprehensively as he wondered what he would actually say when he saw him. *If* he saw him.

"Redfeather. Is that an Indian name?"

"Yeah."

"Sweet. So you're an Indian? Like, uh, what tribe? I mean, what nation?"

"Apache."

Chas was filled with awe-tinged envy. He turned his head and stared appreciatively. Long enough to make Ramie nervous. He wished Chas would keep his eyes on the road.

"No shit? Full-blooded?" Chas asked.

Ramie shook his head. "I'm a half-er. My mother's Irish. Or Scottish. Something." He shrugged. He was pretty tired of his mother.

"So that's where you get the hair. Freaking awesome, dude."

Ramie nodded. "What about you?"

"My tribe is the Undead. I'm running like hell; I'm looking for a new clan. I fucking hate zombies."

"You don't sound like a zombie. Zombies don't talk, and you talk like the wind." Ramie had never met anyone who could talk as much as Chas.

"Oh, zombies talk well enough. But I don't think they're my real family. They can't be. It must've been a case of babies being switched in the nursery. And yeah, I was born talking." He smiled and adjusted the brim of his new hat, sneaking a peak at himself in the rearview mirror.

Ramie allowed a smile to spread across his face.

"How old are you?" Chas glanced over like he was trying to guess. "Are you legal?"

Ramie thought about lying or stretching the truth, but why bother? "Fifteen. Almost sixteen."

"I would've thought you were older. I'm seventeen, but I've got fake ID. You got ID, right? So we can get into this bar—what's it called? Ziggies?"

Ramie nodded, patting his pocket.

"And where exactly is Ziggies?"

Ramie pulled the scrap of paper from his pocket. "On Thirty-Eighth Avenue."

"Cross street?"

"Yates."

Chas unplugged the iPod and plugged in the GPS sitting next to it. "This shit rocks," he said, zooming in on the electronic map.

"Look out!" Ramie shouted as the car veered into the other lane. A horn blared its warning.

"Blow it out your ass, bee-atch! OK, Ramie, you're riding shotgun; you do the navigation. Enter the coordinates."

"I don't know how," Ramie admitted, his cheeks growing hot. "I've never worked one. Where'd you get this car, anyway?"

"I stole it."

"What? You can't steal a classic car like this and get away with it."

"I stole it from my grandma."

Ramie laughed out loud. "No way. And she's letting you drive it all over the country?"

"I didn't ask her." Chas grinned, revealing his crooked teeth.

"So you stole your granny's Cadillac." Ramie shook his head.

"It's not like I'm going to sell it or wreck it or anything. I'm going to bring it back eventually. Besides, I left her a note."

"Yeah, right. That makes everything cool." Ramie remembered the note he left his mother, a note she wouldn't read for hours. His little brother would probably find it first and call Mom at the restaurant, just for the chance to rat him off.

Chas lowered the window to flick his ashes. "See, Gran thinks I'm doing a college interview trip. That's the reason I gave for taking the Caddie out of the garage. I call her every now and then with an update."

"So she's OK with it?"

"Are you kidding me? She's furious. Said she was going to call the cops, but I don't think she did. How could she? She's the one who wants me to go to college. Anyway, the old lady's got other things on her mind."

Ramie didn't ask what she might have on her mind. He didn't really want to know. This guy talked enough already without asking him complicated questions.

"Suddenly, I'm thirsty," announced Chas. "How about you? Want a drink?"

Ramie shrugged. "Sure. What do you got?"

Chas grinned. "I'm hauling a wine cellar in my trunk. Red or white? Varietal or blend?"

Wine?" Ramie had a vague memory of puking pink chunks all over somebody's carpet one night after getting shit-faced on Boone's Farm. It hadn't been a very fun experience.

"I got six cases in the trunk. Vintage Bordeaux, Burgundy, Napa, and Barolo. We're talking hundred-dollar-a-bottle and up. Good shit."

Wine was an old lady's drink. Ramie had been hoping for a cold beer. Or a pull of whiskey. Red Bull and Jagermeister. Anything but wine.

"I can't believe you stole your granny's car—*and* her wine?" he said.

"Are you kidding? Gran's got, like, a thousand bottles in her wine cellar, and most of them are covered with dust. I doubt she'll miss a few cases. She'll probably think she drank it herself; her memory isn't so great. Let's make a pit stop. We'll quench our thirst, get a little happy, and I'll show you how to program the GPS."

Chas stepped on the brakes and swerved onto the next exit, a short ramp that brought them sliding to a stop at a gravel road at right angles to the highway. To the east, over the rise, lay the settlement of Carr, according to the sign.

"What's in Carr?"

Ramie shrugged. "Nuthin'." He had never been to Carr.

"Then we'll go west; we'll follow the sun. 'Go West, young man, go West'—Horace Greeley said that. You ever been to Greeley?"

"Huh-uh. But I heard it smells like cow shit. They got a big slaughterhouse there."

Chas turned westward, throwing up a spray of stones. Ahead of them the sun was a red and swollen face. Chas flicked his ashes out of the window. "Look at these wide open spaces! I expect to see a herd of bison appear any minute. Cowboys and Indians or some shit. What do they do here, brother? What do they do with all this land? Who owns it? Back east it would be all developed into houses and cul-de-sacs, Home Depots, PetSmarts, 7-Elevens, Starbucks, Bob Evanses, you name it. I haven't seen a Bob Evans in days. Who is Bob Evans, anyway? And all this land, what do they do with it?"

"It's just land." Ramie felt like he was finally going somewhere, like he had jumped an invisible fence. He felt like a coyote loping along, sniffing for a jackrabbit. If only this guy would quit talking.

"I wanna be a cowboy, baby…" Chas rapped Kid Rock's number as he pulled off onto the grassy shoulder, narrowly avoiding the drainage ditch. "Gotta piss like a Triple Crown racehorse. Like Secretariat, like Seattle Slew, baby!" He jumped out of the car, unzipped his pants, and relieved himself—a grand arc of urine shimmering golden in the late afternoon sunshine. "Whoo-whee! Colo-fucking-rado! Holy shit—look how far I can piss at this altitude! Out of the ballpark, baby!"

They sat on the hood of the Cadillac, drinking a warm bottle of 1986 Romanee-Conti and smoking a joint that Chas rolled from his small stash. He had heard pot was legal in Colorado. All was quiet except for the dribbling noises of the radiator and the distant whine of traffic on the interstate, a mile to the east, over the rise. Chas could not bear the stillness. With his camera phone, he snapped some photos of the wine bottle on the hood of the car and sent them to Patrick. *What u r missin dude—me getting FUW/ Native!!! An original American!!! AAS*

Chas pocketed the phone and passed the roach to Ramie, who was thinking of his mother. Not that he was missing her; he was just worried what she would do once she read his note. He should call her so she wouldn't worry and do something rash, like call the law. Dude had a cell phone, an iPhone, no less. Maybe he'd let him make a call.

Chas talked like the wind, on and on. A lot of it was just showing off. But whatever. The more Chas talked, the less Ramie had to. It relieved him of a burden. At the same time, the warm wine and sweet weed numbed his head, loosened the coil of thoughts and desires, releasing them into his bloodstream.

"Get out your guitar and play something," Chas said.

"Nah." Ramie passed him back the twist of paper; there was one hit left.

"What do you mean, nah? We've got a moment here, a guitar moment. You need to play a few riffs before we go on. This is like a movie. We need some music, the score, the soundtrack, you know?"

"Need new strings."

Chas pulled an impatient face. "Who cares? It's just you and me."

Ramie shrugged. "I care."

"I don't know why you're carrying it all the way to Denver if you're not going to play it. We can find a Guitar City and get you some new strings."

Ramie just shook his head. How to tell this guy, this intrusive, diarrhea-of-the-mouth stranger, that this particular guitar wasn't something you just messed around on? The time had to be right; he didn't play on demand. Actually, he wasn't very good. Yet. The guitar was more a talisman than a musical instrument.

"I'm thinking about calling my band Excoriation," Ramie said. "Or Hell Hounds Unleashed. When I start a band, that is. When I'm good enough."

"That's cool. I like those names." Chas inhaled the last bit of the joint before crushing it under the heel of his high-top Cons. He wished he played an instrument, keyboard maybe. Harmonica. Or drums. He wished he had a pair of cowboy boots to go with his hat. He wished he had a double cheeseburger with bacon and a large order of fries. And a chocolate shake.

They passed the bottle back and forth as the sun set behind the purple mountains, sending out wide rays and coloring the clouds extravagantly with swaths of pink and orange. Then Chas forgot about the cowboy boots and the bacon cheeseburger, and for a minute, for sixty full seconds, he wanted nothing and had nothing to say.

5

They flashed their fake IDs, handed over three crumpled dollar bills each, and sidled in, losing themselves in the crowd. Back by the pool table, two women were playing a game of eight ball. The corner stage was empty but for a house amplifier and microphone stand. A spotlight shone on it expectantly. It was like a party in somebody's basement— except most of the guests were old enough to be their parents. Or grandparents.

"Redfeather playing tonight?" Chas asked the waitress carrying a foaming mug of beer in each hand. She wasn't old; she was hot. She wore a pink-and-orange-striped T-shirt that reminded him of Nemo. Her shapely legs were swathed in tight denim, and she wore pink running shoes with lime-green laces.

"That's the rumor."

"I'd like a Coors, when you get a chance," he said boldly.

Ramie cringed. Nobody he knew in Cheyenne drank Coors, even though it was made in the neighboring state, in Golden, Colorado. "I'll have a Bud." He waited for the pink-shoed waitress to ask for their IDs, but she didn't.

Ramie's eyes searched the room, trying to take it all in. His gaze fell upon a folded card on a nearby table cluttered with empty glasses and the remains of a plate of nachos. He picked it up.

His heart flopped like a fish out of water. What would he say? He had no idea. Ramie pocketed the card.

Chas lingered by the pool table, pretending to watch the game. Eric Clapton on the sound system singing "Cocaine" reminded him of his father. Charles Sr. was a major fan of both Clapton and cocaine. The feeling crept over Chas again, the feeling that he was living in somebody else's shadow, that his life didn't really count for much. He took another swallow of beer and felt his head tilt and spin, which made him think of a carnival ride, the Tilt-a-Whirl. He was ready to ride until his head flew off.

Nine o'clock came and went, but still no Redfeather. The corner stage remained empty and dark; the sound system continued to play satellite radio, classic blues and rock. Chas went outside for a smoke, and Ramie recklessly ordered two more beers. What the hell—if they got thrown out now, what did it matter? He was amazed when the waitress brought the beers without question. She was beginning to look frazzled, in an exciting way, her face glistening, her hair falling out of the claw-like clip on the top of her head.

"So, do you know Redfeather?" Ramie blurted out.

"Everybody around here knows Redfeather. Well, actually, I don't know him personally, but I've heard about him. He's, like, a local legend."

Ramie's heart thumped against his chest. "So where is he?"

She shook her head and smiled. "I don't know. Actually, I'm kind of new here. Ask Peggy, the bartender. She'll know." The waitress whirled away to take another drink order.

"Hey, wait—what's your name?" Ramie was surprised by his for-wardness with the woman, who had to be at least twenty-one to be working in a bar. She reminded him of his pretty science teacher—she had the same long, slender legs and breasts like two tennis balls. But the barmaid didn't answer him; she had disappeared, slipping through the crowd.

Sitting in the corner table, Ramie lingered over the beer, thinking about what he would say. His mind was numb, mute. He had come a long way for nothing. But the beer was good, and he had never before in his life been to Denver, Colorado. He sat back and let the roar of voices and the canned music wash over him, working up his courage to go talk to the bartender.

"Got ID, kid?" From behind the bar, Peggy gave him a penetrating stare. Her eyes were like the blue flame that comes from the burner on a gas stove.

Ramie had a feeling she'd recognize his driver's license for the fake it was. "I'm not here to drink. I'm here for the music. I'm here to see Redfeather."

"Ha! You and me and everybody else. What's a sweet young thing like you know about the blues?" She leaned over the bar for a closer look.

Ramie stood tall and strong as a cottonwood. "I came all the way down from Cheyenne to see him."

"OK, now I see the resemblance. Oh, yeah. Uh-huh."

He flinched. The loose, rolling thoughts stopped dead.

"Except for the hair, you favor him. You related? A nephew? His kid brother by another mother maybe?

Ramie felt an electric-like sting, a painful tingle in his arms and legs and on the back of his neck. He swallowed hard.

"Oh my God. I get it. You're his son, ain't you? Where'd you get that hair?"

"My mother, I guess," Ramie said.

"Ray Redfeather is one hell of a musician. How about you, kid? You a musician too? Does it run in the blood?"

He shook his head. His hands tingled. "Not really. I play guitar. A little."

The bartender moved to the cash register to close out a tab, counting out the change.

Ramie waited, letting the noise of the place vibrate his bones, loosen his skin. The dull roar of voices, of drunken laughter. She returned with a glass and set it in front of him.

"Here's a Coke. On the house. I don't know what happened, why he didn't show. Maybe he'll call yet. Say he got his dates crossed or something. It happens. He used to do that to me all the time. Or maybe he'll come draggin' his ass in late and all buzzed up, just like he used to."

Ramie's eyes flew to the door as someone entered, but it was not who he was looking for.

"Go on, now, go away from the bar with your fake ID. The Man come in here, he'll shut us down."

Ramie finished his Coke and slipped outside. There was Chas with three other guys, leaning against the building in a cloud of cigarette smoke.

"What up, bro?"

Ramie was excited, but he couldn't form it into words. "He's good. Lady said he's good." Ramie felt good, real good. Best he felt in a long while. He didn't want to move.

Chas offered him a cigarette. "A little nicotine is what you need. He'll be here, wait and see."

They smoked under the yellow streetlights. The city air was hot and still. Three motorcycles roared by, side by side, like they owned the street. The smell of cigarette smoke hung in the air, not going anywhere.

A yellow taxicab rolled up and stopped in front of the bar. Ramie's heart turned over and played dead for a second. But it wasn't Redfeather who got out of the back seat.

It was a girl——a fair young thing, with a cascade of black hair falling down her back, spilling over her face, a sprite wearing ragged red All-Stars on her child-size feet. All the smokers watched as she handed the driver a bill and with all the moxie of a rock star picked up her guitar case and walked inside. They all dropped their cigarettes in the butt can and followed her.

6

Ramie and Chas stood at the side of the stage, slack-jawed and smitten. What a big voice for such a little thing, barely five feet tall. She had them bewitched; in fact, everyone in the bar was under her spell as she sang Kristofferson's song about being busted flat in Baton Rouge and waiting for a train.

A long fringe of bangs veiled her dark eyes, and she didn't look at a soul, she was lost in the song. (Oh, to be named Bobby McGee, thought Ramie, and to have your name come out of her mouth sounding like that!) She seemed to give herself over to some higher power, some possessive force that contorted her face, jerked her legs, and flung her head from side to side. Her voice was rough, like a cat's tongue on their ears, yet every note was dead-on. The singer had the gift of perfect pitch.

"Thank y'all. My name is LaRoux. Mae B. LaRoux, and I'm from Baton Rouge." The bar crowd clapped heartily for her. She wasn't Redfeather, but she was cute and she gave it her all.

LaRoux accompanied herself on a three-quarter-size Martin acoustic guitar. Her voice was hypnotic; her voice commanded their presence. Her voice struck them dumb, though Chas did have the presence of mind to record the performance on his iPhone and upload it to YouTube, posting a link to his Facebook friends and Twitter followers.

But LaRoux's repertoire was brief. After performing only six songs, the young singer from Baton Rouge bowed and thanked the crowd, who responded with another wave of applause. This time the applause was even louder and punctuated by hoots, whistles, and the stamping of feet.

The young singer had no encore; she had played every song she knew the chords to. But the audience would not let her go—they kept clapping and calling out, "Play some more!" So she started over from the top, singing the same songs she had just finished, singing her heart out. The boys remained at the foot of the stage, entranced. It seemed every word out of her mouth was for them.

Fifteen minutes later she took her final bow, her face flushed and shining with satisfaction. The clapping died away, replaced by the dull roar of talk, laughter, the smack of pool balls. From behind the bar, Peggy turned on the stereo, and Tom Petty sang about free-fallin' in Reseda down Ventura Boulevard.

The girl was returning her guitar to its case when Chas tapped her on the shoulder.

"What are you drinking, Miss LaRoux? 'Cause I'm buying. You were amazing!"

"Ice tea, please," she croaked. "I'm fairly dying of thirst!"

"Ice tea? You got it."

Ramie shifted his weight to his other foot, feeling awkward, trying to think of something entertaining to say. Something that would make her smile. But he could think of nothing. Meanwhile Chas went to the bar and brought back a glass of ice water; there was no tea to be had. He offered the sweating glass to the singer like it was a chalice of mead.

She took a long pull. "I'm not used to singing so long. That was my first encore! So exciting!" She pronounced it *ex-satin*. Her eyes shone.

"That calls for a celebration," Chas said. "I've got some Dom Perignon in the trunk. It's warm, but—what do you say?"

"Pardon me? It's a little loud in here."

"I've got something more suitable than beer or ice tea to celebrate your performance and your first encore. Would you accompany me to my tasting room?"

Her laugh was a rush of sound, like water gurgling over rocks.

"Can I carry your guitar?"

"I've got it," said Ramie, nudging Chas aside.

"You can carry my backpack if you want," she said. "I'd appreciate it. What did y'all say your names was?"

"My name's Chas." *And I'm in love*, he thought.

"Ramie. Pleased to meet you, Miss LaRoux." Ramie's insides were as soft as a tub of margarine left out on the counter.

The cork shot up like a rocket, and warm champagne spewed out of the bottle, spraying them with mist. The three sat on the hood of the Caddie and passed the bottle, sharing their stories, somewhat shined up and rewritten on the fly. They talked about their travels, where they were from, and how long they had been on the road. Even Ramie was finding it easier to talk, his thoughts shaken free by alcohol—and the ready acceptance of benevolent strangers, two people he had known less than six hours.

"So you see, we're on a mission," Chas was saying. "A quest, of sorts. We're looking for Redfeather, Ramie's father, gone missing, since, what, birth?"

Ramie nodded, thinking that Chas made it sound like an epic movie, like *Lord of the Rings* or something.

"Me, I'm doing the college tour thing," Chas continued. "And getting the hell out of Baltimore for the summer. It's freaking hot back there, and nothing happens, no good concerts this year. But what about you, Mae B. LaRoux? By the way, love the name!"

"Do you?" She beamed. "I made it up."

"No way! What's your real name, dare I ask?"

"Mae B. LaRoux *is* my real name. But if you must know, my birth certificate says Faith Appleby." She made a face.

"I like Faith," Ramie said. "Faith is pretty."

"Forget Faith, got it?" She looked at him, snapping her fingers with mock sternness.

He marveled at her hands, the slender pointed fingers, the tiny, chewed-down nails, polish chipped away to fragments of midnight blue. "Forget what name?" Ramie quipped, pleased with his comeback.

"So Mae B., baby, I hope you don't mind, I posted my video of you on YouTube." Chas said, eager to win back her attentions.

The girl flipped back a strand of dark hair and gave him a flirtatious smile. "No, I don't mind. Y'all are the captains of my fan club, 'K?"

"Oh yeah. That I am. Love your accent, darlin'." Everything about this girl was cool, was hot, was absolutely amazing. "What brings you to Denver? You on tour?"

She sighed. "Actually, I'm just starting out. I'm looking to be discovered. I need a paying gig before I go to Austin to compete in the Break Out Blues Contest. See, my parents think I'm a counselor at summer Bible camp, but even if they find out the truth, what can they do? I'm sixteen." She stated the fact with such assuredness, it made Ramie shiver. "At sixteen you don't run away from home so much as you just let the wind pick you up and take you. Know what I mean?"

Ramie was not going to admit that he had not yet reached that milestone. Fifteen was pathetic compared to sixteen.

Chas reached for his cigarettes and offered one to LaRoux.

"No, thank you. I don't smoke," she said. "Until tonight I never drank champagne. Y'all are the first wine connoisseurs I ever met."

"Hell, he's no connoisseur," Ramie blurted out, envious of Chas, his apparent wealth, his gift of gab. "He stole this shit from his granny."

"Whatever. It's my inheritance," Chas said. "I'm spending it now, I'm sharing it with friends. Gran would want that, she loves me."

LaRoux burst out laughing, that lovely waterfalling gurgle, and Ramie laughed too. How could he not? Chas really was entertaining, and Chas made it easier, made it possible even, to be sitting here on the hood of a vintage Cadillac with this amazing girl.

"So what are y'all's plans?"

"Oh, we don't make plans, we live for the moment," Chas quipped.

"Well, I make plans. Where are y'all staying?"

Chas turned to look at Ramie; they had neither one thought of where they would sleep. Chas had spent four hours last night sleeping in the car, parked in a brightly lit rest stop on Interstate 80.

"We just got into Denver. We don't even have a lay of the land yet," Chas said, blowing a stream of smoke into the air. "Do you have lodging, Miss LaRoux? Someplace we can take you?"

"No." She sighed. "I don't know. I got a sleeping bag. There's a bicycle path that runs through the city. Runs along a river. Lot of folks camp along there, under the bridges. I heard about it on the bus. In Kansas City I slept in a church doorway the first night, then I found a hostel. I think I liked the church doorway better."

Chas marveled at her boldness. He had been sleeping in the car, but there wasn't room for all three of them, and it might be a little awkward. Maybe he should get them a room, or two rooms, but motels were expensive, and he didn't have all that much left in his bank account. It was a warm night and camping would be fun.

Sitting there watching the cars go by on Thirty-Eighth Avenue, Ramie's head swirled. His life had taken a drastic change of course in the past few hours. What speed! He couldn't seem to corral the excitement, the disappointment, the crazy-wild thoughts stampeding his brain.

Ramie was disappointed he hadn't found his father like he had set out to do. But he had stumbled onto something unexpected, something he couldn't walk away from. It was like a door had appeared—an open-ing, a wormhole to a new universe. Who knew what would happen next? The world was his highway, and life was a stolen Cadillac. Ramie Redfeather had stuck out his thumb and hitched himself a ride.

7

The South Platte River was really more of a stream, Chas thought as he nestled into his sleeping bag, thumbs busy on the iPod screen. The so-called river began high in the Rocky Mountains and meandered through Denver on its way north and east to the plains of Nebraska where it joined the North Platte to become the Platte River—which was a tributary of the Missouri River, which was a tributary of the mighty Mississippi, the highway of all rivers. Long before there were roads, people followed streams of water, Chas realized with a new appreciation. The Arapaho Indians used to camp on the banks of the South Platte, he read on his pocket encyclopedia. They traded with fur trappers who navigated the West by following rivers long before highways or railroads connected the country. Maybe some of them camped here, on this very spot.

It was a sketchy area, with an air of neglect about it. Here, the South Platte ran through an industrial section, abandoned at night except for transients. People like them. In the old days, they might have been called hobos or tramps, but now these itinerants were called "the homeless." *Homeless* was a derogatory term, he thought; it made them sound less than people who paid rent or were in debt for life to pay mortgages on permanent dwellings. The Indians were mobile, and so were the trappers and gold miners. What was a home anyway?

Chas had parked his car at a truck stop, and the three of them had walked a short distance across the lot to the bike path that followed the river. Nearby, they could see makeshift campsites: cardboard boxes and plastic tarps strung from trees. Chas led them in the other direction until they found a suitable clearing. Kicking aside empty bottles from previous campers, they made their beds on the lush sedge and blue stem grasses growing by the stream.

Beside him, LaRoux snuggled into her sleeping bag, the same one she had been taking to Bible camp every year since she was twelve years old. She could smell the rich dampness of the river mud and the ripeness of the crushed plants beneath her. She felt safe between her new-found friends, and her guardian angel perched in the branches of the willow overhead. Her head swimming in champagne, she closed her eyes and relaxed, listening to the peeping of frogs. The sound reminded her of home.

On the other side of LaRoux, Ramie stretched out, wrapped in the couch throw he had taken from home, his backpack for a pillow. He was thrilled to be sleeping next to a girl, but he was also exhausted. And more than a little drunk.

"Did you guys know the Arapaho Indians once camped here, before the city of Denver was ever even dreamed of?"

Chas's words hung in the air, unanswered. His friends were already asleep. His phone died in his hand, and he was alone. Lying perfectly still he listened to the gurgle of running water and the hum of traffic on the crisscross of highways and boulevards nearby. He felt wary and in some way responsible for the safety of his new friends. His hand felt for the knife deep in his right pocket, just in case someone came along and tried to fuck with them. But it was late, and all seemed quiet.

Chas marveled at his uncanny luck in seeing a hitchhiker that afternoon—and at his daring decision to stop for him. Ever since he got his driver's license Chas had been warned never to pick up hitchhikers—but if he hadn't stopped for Ramie, his life would be completely different right now. He'd disobeyed a sensible rule and had been rewarded for it. He might have just as easily been killed.

Every action, every choice you made, altered your course. Each person you met could change you in some way, and you could change them. There was no going back. You couldn't undo something. You couldn't put your life in reverse to fix a mistake; you could only go forward. If he hadn't stopped for Ramie, he wouldn't have met LaRoux and they wouldn't be here now. But was it free will and luck—or was it fate? Was it free will that made you responsible for everything that happened to you? Or was there a God who was directing everything? What if he, Chas, was merely a puppet in a scripted cosmic play? And if so, who was the audience? Could it be that free will and destiny somehow worked together? Trying to wrap his alcohol-befuddled brain around these unanswerable questions was too much, and Chas finally gave in to the crushing oblivion of sleep, the deep, total sleep of a seventeen-year-old.

Through the bushes a red fox watched them curiously, and overhead an owl flew on silent wings.

They woke hungry and thirsty, with pounding heads and bad breath. The sun was bright and hot and drove them out of their sleeping bags.

"Don't drink the stream water, it might be polluted," Chas warned.

"Y'all want some gum?" LaRoux rummaged through her pack.

They peed in the bushes, packed up their bedding, and headed for the car, where Chas charged up his phone and consulted the electronic map of Denver. LaRoux combed her hair and put on eyeliner using the rearview mirror while Ramie crashed out in the backseat.

"Where are we going, Chas?"

"Colfax, baby. The longest street in the world."

Colfax Avenue was an exciting mash-up of ethnic restaurants, liquor stores, tattoo parlors, nightclubs, and marijuana clinics advertising weed by prescription with neon green crosses. In the midst of all the seedy commercialism shone the brilliant gold dome of the state capitol building, resplendent in the high-noon sun. You could see the Rocky Mountains in the distance, a faint trace of snow on the highest peaks. Chas figured those mountains were miles away—what, sixty miles maybe? And yet there they were, free for the looking.

Chas found free parking in Argonaut Liquor Store's lot. "Let's find us some breakfast."

They walked three abreast, unaware of the other pedestrians stepping aside for them. It was as if they were surrounded by a thin film, a large soap bubble. At any moment they might rise off the ground and float up into the clear, thin air. At the stoplight on the corner of Colfax and Pearl Street, Chas pulled out his phone, cupping his hand over the screen to shield it from the sunlight.

"Colfax is the longest *commercial* avenue in the world, according to Wikipedia. More than twenty-six miles. Named after President Ulysses S. Grant's vice president. Oh, and Jack Kerouac spent time in Denver. He wrote about Colfax."

Blank looks. Simultaneous *whatevers* expressed in body language.

"Jack Kerouac. You know, *On the Road?* The Beat Generation?"

They did not know.

"Oh, come on! You have got to know *On the Road.*" Chas pocketed his iPhone and lit up a cigarette. "*On the Road* is a literary classic."

"Was it a movie?" LaRoux asked.

"No. Well, they might have made it into a movie; I don't know." He drew on the cigarette impatiently. "*On the Road* is an iconic American story. Written in the 1950s. Or maybe it was the '60s."

Their eyes glazed over; he was losing them.

"The author, Jack Kerouac, he was one of the Beat Generation."

"Is that, like, the Beatles?" LaRoux asked politely.

Chas sighed. "No, darlin'. The Beatles were a British band. Jack Kerouac was an American. A novelist. He went on a road trip with some friends and wrote about everything that happened to them."

Chas had never actually read Kerouac's novel—but he knew about it. It was part of American culture. His new friends were blank slates. Ignorant as savages. But maybe he was too hung up in the past. After all, Jack Kerouac was his grandmother's generation. Fuck Kerouac; he would write his own story. He would write his own novel. He would write a screenplay that would reveal the new century through his own eyes and ears. He would become famous for it. He would be the voice of the new generation…

"You should quit those evil cancer sticks," LaRoux scolded him, jabbing him in the side with her elbow. "They'll be the death of you."

"You're right. I should quit." Chas grinned. He liked the way she narrowed her eyes and flashed her tiny teeth, a sparkle of silver on her tongue. His side tingled where she had elbowed him, and the effervescence spread throughout his body, like his blood had magically become champagne.

LaRoux was quite unlike any girl he had ever met. She seemed at once mature yet childlike. Unlearned, unspoiled by education and popular culture, as if she had been raised in a convent. Now sprung free, she dressed carelessly, as if she wanted to hide her femininity. She wore baggy camo pants with oversized cargo pockets, a wrinkled black T-shirt worn inside out. A cross on a silver chain hung down between her breasts, bumps like apricots beneath the shirt. Her nails were bitten to

the quick. Those bitten, blue fingernails melted his heart, as did the silver stud in her tongue that glistened like a dewdrop when she laughed.
Most thrilling of all was the predominantly green, vine-like tattoo that
started at her right elbow, disappeared under her sleeve, and reappeared
on the left side of her neck, half-hidden by her jet-black hair. Chas wanted so much to touch it, to trace it with his finger.

"Nice ink," he said.

"You like it?" LaRoux smiled. "I got it in Kansas City."

"What is it? Looks like some sort of foliage."

"No, silly. That's just part of it. Actually, it's a leopard. Most of it is
hidden under my T-shirt. "

"Sweet!"

"Wait—there's a leopard under your shirt?" Ramie blurted out, un-
able to contain his curiosity. "Can we see it?"

"Not all of it!" LaRoux looked from one boy to the other, beaming.
"She's hiding just under my sleeve."

Chas too, was hoping to see more of the tattoo. "Here, kitty, kitty,
kitty."

LaRoux lifted her right sleeve to reveal the face of a big cat bar-
ing its fangs. It reminded him somewhat of the Cheshire cat of *Alice in
Wonderland*. Chas, who had no tattoos on his freckled, pimpled skin, felt
generic. Plain and ordinary.

"Stop! Right there!" He reached into his pocket for his iPhone. "I
want your picture, both of you; I want to capture this moment. I want
to record LaRoux giving us a glimpse of her tattoo. Ready? Three, two,
one—go."

LaRoux pulled up her T-shirt sleeve to reveal her inked bicep and
winked, then flipped back her hair and bared her teeth with a cat-like
hiss.

"Oh yeah! Now flex that muscle, sweet thing. Yeah, that's what I'm
talking about! I love this! Hey Ramie, stand next to LaRoux. That's it.

OK, I'm switching to video. We're here on Colfax, where Jack Kerouac once walked. I'm going to post this all over the Internet. I'm going to blog this—no—I'm going to make a documentary about us. About Mae B. LaRoux and Ramie Looking-for-Redfeather and Chas Sweeney, a man on the run." *Band on the run.* The words to the old Paul McCartney song filled his head, a head so filled with songs and images and ideas it felt ready to burst.

"You have to photoshop my face so my parents don't recognize me," LaRoux said, giggling. "Not that they ever watch YouTube."

Chas ducked in beside her, close enough to smell her hair, like ripe pears drizzled with honey.

"Heads together, bitches. Let's see some cheese!"

Holding the camera phone in his hand, he extended it as far in front of them as his arm would reach. "Live on Colfax Avenue in the mile-high city of Denver, Colorado!"

They made outrageous faces, sticking out their tongues and rolling their eyes. Ramie raised his arms high, folding his fingers in the pronged heavy-metal salute. A passing car sounded its horn, and they thought it was for them, approval for their spontaneous street performance. Colfax Avenue was a stage, and they were the stars of the show.

Chas had no time to upload the video. His imagined audience would have to wait. He had no time to blog or to text his friends back home because Ramie and LaRoux were already ahead of him, walking down the sidewalk, arm in arm. They were here, now. The three of them were alive; they were fluid, ever-changing, moving on, and he had to keep up. He had to lead; he was the leader. His online friends—who were they but avatars? Stupid, tasteless profile pictures, suggestive comments left on his page and instantly forgotten. Virtual opponents he played video games with were nothing more than imaginary friends. None of them were in the flesh. Even Patrick, whom he had known since third grade and had left at O'Hare airport less than forty-eight hours ago, was a ghost from another lifetime. Chas pocketed his phone and hurried to catch up.

Ramie, LaRoux, and Chas—their faces shone with expectation of that unknown thing, that emotion, that event, that revealed truth that would throw open the door to the universe. Their bodies radiated energy; they were triple stars caught in each other's orbits. They were expanding, heating up; like supernovae, they were about to explode.

A woman in a leopard-print bathrobe driving an electric wheelchair asked for a cigarette. Her mouth was a blur of orange. The bathrobe reminded Chas of LaRoux's leopard tattoo, and he gave the woman the rest of his pack.

"There," he announced to LaRoux as they continued on. "I've quit. For you, darlin'. Happy now?"

LaRoux narrowed her eyes and shook her finger. "What are you thinking, giving that poor woman your coffin nails? What kind of help is that, Chas Sweeney?"

Chas melted under her scolding. The three linked arms, LaRoux in the middle. The boys lifted her by the elbows and carried her down the sidewalk as she screamed to be put down. But she didn't mean it, and they knew it. She loved being the center of their attention.

"Hey, kid! Got any matches?" the lady with the orange mouth called after them. "What good are smokes without a light?" But they didn't hear her; they had moved on and were out of her orbit.

Ramie borrowed Chas's phone and dropped back a few steps to make his call, watching his new friends, arm in arm and laughing.

"Hi, Mom."

"Where are you? I've been worried sick. I was just about to call the police."

"No, don't do that! I'm fine, Mom. Really."

"Well? Did you find him?"

"No. But I found the place where he was supposed to play last night. Except he never showed up. Something bad might have happened."

He heard her sigh, blowing air out through her nose. "You need to get back here, Ramie. You can't run off like this. I don't want to have to call the cops to bring you home."

"Don't do that, Mom. No need to call the cops. I'm fine. I met up with some guys. Chas and LaRoux. Chas has a car."

"Wait, where are you?"

"Denver."

"It sounds like you're standing in the middle of the street!"

"Yeah, it's traffic noise. I'm on Colfax Avenue." He was amazed to hear himself say that.

"Look here, Ramie, you need to get home. You don't have any money—except what you took from my tip jar." Her voice rose, he could feel her anger. "And what about Brandon? Who is going to watch your little brother while I'm at work? I need you here, mister."

Ramie heard himself shouting. "Brandon's old enough to watch himself. You left me alone when I was ten. He doesn't listen to me anyway, the little shit."

"You leave me no choice but to call the cops and tell them my fifteen-year-old son has run away. They'll pick your ass up, they'll—"

"No! Mom, don't call the cops. Do *not* call the cops, OK? I'm not a runaway; I'm talking to you, aren't I? I called *you*, right?"

"Ramie, do you realize you have a court date in two weeks?"

"I know, Mom. That's why you can't rat me out. You don't want them to put me away in juvie hall, do you?"

"It's just—Denver is so far away, Ramie. It's a big city, and bad things can happen. Christ, I've got enough to worry about without you pulling another stupid stunt like this."

"Mom. I can take care of myself; I'm almost sixteen. I'm looking for Redfeather—I have to. I have to do this thing."

There was silence on the other end, and Ramie didn't know if he had lost the signal or if his mother had ended the conversation and was calling the cops. "Mom?"

There was no answer.

Ramie caught up with his friends in a few easy strides. "Here's your phone, Chas. Got the old woman off my back for a while." But he looked nervously over his shoulder, as if he expected to see flashing blue lights.

"Thanks, bro." Chas thought about calling Gran or sending her another text for reassurance. But later. He'd do it later. He couldn't bear to think about his family right now. Chas Sweeney was hungry. In fact, he was starving.

8

Across the street a restaurant materialized before their eyes. Tom's Diner.

"Let's eat," said Chas.

The blast of cool air felt refreshing against their skin, and the smell of bacon frying was tantalizing. Big, old-fashioned, over-stuffed booths, the bright color of taxi cabs. Eighties music filled the room. Foreigner singing, "I wanna know what love is"—that's just how they felt! Lyrics and music composed and recorded long before they were born had been given new significance. Everything they saw and heard seemed important, meaningful, created for them alone.

"Breakfast is on me, my friends," Chas said largely. "Have whatever you want."

They took him at his word, ordering as if money were no object, as if they had just returned, triumphant, from a long and arduous journey. A waitperson brought them coffee (a man or a woman, they weren't sure), and they admired the sinewy arm, a panorama of ink from wrist to armpit. Chas felt like he was in some kind of spontaneous street performance and everyone they saw was a character.

Bacon—a pile of bacon, stacked like firewood—and hash browns, steaming beneath the brown crust. Heaps of fluffy scrambled eggs, golden pancakes, stacks of buttered white toast. Ice tea, chocolate milk, orange juice, and coffee served in thick mugs, cracked from years of holding hot coffee, mugs that had touched how many lips? *More coffee? Oh yes, please*, and Chas shoveled in the sugar, stirring the muddy slurry, appreciating for the first time how good coffee could be.

They ate with great pleasure, devouring only what they liked and as much of it as they wanted with no one to tell them to go easy on the milk. For LaRoux it was her first real date—a double date, at that—and she felt grown up at last, having breakfast in a diner in Denver after doing a gig and sleeping under the stars with two boys. She borrowed Chas's phone and texted Jordan to make sure everything was OK, and her friend texted back *Alls well—so far. Miss u!*

Chas was a compulsive reader. He liked to read at the table; as a child he read the back of cereal boxes, Gran's old newspapers. Now, between forks of spongy pancake soaked in maple syrup, he surfed the Internet on his phone, his fingers flying. He was reading about Apaches.

"Dude! Do you think you might be descended from Cochise? Is this possible?"

Ramie shrugged. "Maybe. I like the song 'Cochise.' You know, Audioslave?"

"Hell, yeah, I love Audioslave! I can't believe Cornell left the band, it won't be the same." Even as he talked, Chas searched the Internet. He brought up a new screen, reading aloud from Wikipedia. "In an interview, guitarist Tom Morello said this about the song: 'Cochise was the last great American Indian chief to die free and absolutely unconquered.'"

"That's badass," said Ramie, gulping the last of his chocolate milk. He felt an inexplicable little burst of pride.

Chas continued to surf, his fingers sliding over the screen with the dexterity of those of a blind man reading braille. "And listen to this. Victorio—you know Victorio, the Apache warrior? Says here he was of the Chihenne band of the Chiricahua Apaches and is believed to have kinship ties with the Navajo. Oh, and LaRoux, get this. Victorio had a sister." His eyes flew over the screen, drinking the information, turning it into muscle and bone. "She was a warrior, she fought alongside the men. And she was said to have had special powers—supernatural powers. She knew where the enemy was, from what direction they were approaching."

"That's cool. What was her name?"

"Let's see." He scanned the screen. "Her name was Lozen. Says here she was a warrior woman."

"Lozen," she said, savoring the word, enjoying the way it sounded. "I want that name. I want to be Lozen. Forget Mae B. I'm Lozen, got it? From now on, I'm Lozen LaRoux."

"I was just starting to get used to Mae B.," said Chas.

"Well, I changed my mind. I don't like it anymore. Mae B. is too old, too Southern. Too Mae B. Sue. Mae B. Sue LaRoux." She pulled a pouty face that won them both.

"OK, whatever you want, Lozen. But honestly, I like the name Faith. The name you were born with."

"So do I," said Ramie.

"Don't y'all call me Faith." She looked sternly from one to the other. "Faith is no more."

They nodded solemnly then were completely surprised as she leaned across the table and planted a swift kiss on each unsuspecting mouth.

"You are my Apache brothers, and I am your sister, Lozen."

Neither Chas nor Ramie wanted to be LaRoux's brother. But it was a start. At least they were on equal footing. She had kissed them. She had called them brother. They were a tribe of three.

The check came and Chas paid with his debit card, adding on a generous tip, hoping like hell his grandmother would deposit some more money into his dwindling account.

9

In spite of the euphoria of his newly found freedom, Ramie felt the disappointment of his failure to find his father, which was why he had left home in the first place. He had been on a mission, and the mission had failed. The disappointment was working its way into his soul like a piece of gravel stuck in his shoe; he could feel it with every step, and it bothered him, but he didn't want to stop long enough to shake it out. If he stopped, he might be left behind.

Ziggies had been a bust. The man called Redfeather was a vanishing act, a myth. But the bartender had said he was good, and the crowd that had come to see him and hear him—well, that said something, didn't it? Redfeather was some sort of urban legend in Denver. Redfeather— his own last name. It made Ramie proud to know his father was talented and nearly a celebrity. Maybe he hadn't shown up at Ziggies last night because he had lined up a bigger, better gig. Maybe he was in Los Angeles, recording a new release. Maybe he was in Hollywood.

"See, Redfeather is like a minstrel," said Chas. "He's a bard, an American Homer." He wanted to make Ramie feel better about not meeting his father last night, and he wanted to keep the hope alive.

LaRoux admired Chas's vocabulary. He used words like *minstrel* and *bard*, though she wasn't sure about Homer. Homer wasn't musical at all, to her way of thinking. She had never been allowed to watch *The Simpsons* television show, but she had seen episodes on YouTube. Everybody knew *The Simpsons*. Homer and Marge reminded her of her own parents.

Chas was going on again, spilling random facts, sweeping his head clean. He was saying how musicians and storytellers once traveled great distances bringing news of wars and natural disasters, making them into ballads and poems set to music. And how before there was television, YouTube, and Netflix, before there were even books and newspapers, these minstrels and bards spread the stories around the countryside. Chas was telling them about the blind Greek poet named Homer who wrote *The Iliad* and *The Odyssey* way back when, like, in the eighth century BC.

"*The Iliad* and *The Odyssey* are the oldest works of literature in Western civilization," said Chas, thinking of the honors literature class he had failed because he never turned in his assignments.

"What are they about?" LaRoux wanted to know.

"Oh, all sorts of things. But mostly it's about these guys who go off to fight the Trojans, and the gods play them like pawns. The gods, the Greek gods, are capricious. All jealous and scheming. Anyway, this one guy named Odysseus—he was a king, I think—he tries to go home after the war. I can't remember all the details, but he gets waylaid a bunch of times and outwits the cyclops and the Lotus Eaters, and he travels by ship, and Aeolus, the wind god, jacks with him, and it takes him, like, I don't know, twenty years to get home. And he's got a son, Telemachus, who all this time tries to keep the suitors away from his mother. Her name is Penelope, and she tricks the suitors—"

"Why does she have to trick them?" LaRoux interrupted. "Why can't she just tell the losers to get lost?"

Chas shrugged. "I don't know. Back in those days women had to be married to somebody; they couldn't just be on their own. Especially a queen, she had to have a king. You couldn't let a powerful position like that go vacant."

LaRoux made a face. "That sucks. It's, like, if you were a girl, you always had to have a boss."

"But that's not the point. The point is all the cool adventures Odysseus has while trying to get back home. And Penelope remains faithful. And his son believes that he'll return."

Ramie thought the story sounded vaguely familiar; he thought there might have been a miniseries about it on TV when he was younger. He liked to think of his father as being on some twenty-year voyage, trying to get back home to Cheyenne. But Ramie had not done his job in keeping the suitors away from Penelope, not at all. He had failed his father miserably.

He had also failed his mother and his little brother. He was needed to babysit Brandon when their mother had to work late at the restaurant, several nights a week and always on a Friday and Saturday night. Ramie resented that. After all, Brandon had a father. Hap came by now and again and took his kid for the weekend, but there was no set schedule. Sometimes he even took Ramie too, mostly so Hap and his girlfriend could go out to the bars. They'd pay Ramie to babysit Brandon and Corrine, the girlfriend's kid, a bossy little princess who cried if she didn't get to watch *Zack & Cody* on the Disney Channel or if Ramie tried to make her go to bed early. *I get to stay up as late as I want, my mom said.* It almost wasn't worth the five dollars he got. Except for the fringe benefits. Like Hap's liquor cabinet.

Ramie had discovered Wild Turkey at Hap's. He never drank enough for him to notice, but then Hap went through a lot of Wild Turkey; he bought it like most people buy milk or orange juice. Ramie never drank enough to get sick-drunk, the way he had the first time with another of his mother's boyfriends—what was his name, Roy? Randy? Whatever his name was, he had tried to win Ramie over, tried to be cool, pouring him a little shot when Mom wasn't looking, hooking him up with a little pot now and then during the early days of the relationship. The courting days, the *Hey, pretty mama, I like your kids, I'd love to be their stepdad if you'll let me sleep in your bed* days. Those days never seemed to last very long—and neither did the boyfriends. Was his mother such a bitch? Did she drive them all away with her impossible demands? Or did they not want to be bothered with punk kids who weren't their own?

Whatever. That was just fine with Ramie and Brandon; it was the one thing they agreed upon. They didn't need any of Mom's boyfriends moving in and taking over the couch, the remote control, the refrigerator, the bathroom. Like they owned it all. They didn't need some man moving his shit in, getting mean-drunk or tweaked out on meth and changing the rules, making their lives all kinds of hell. That was one thing he and Brandon agreed on. No live-in boyfriends. No stepfathers for them.

Maybe he should forget about finding Redfeather. Maybe he should head on back home to Cheyenne. He could hop on a bus or stick out his thumb, the same way he got to Denver. He should be there to keep Brandon in line; the little punk could get out of hand. Who was Redfeather to him anyhow? What had Redfeather ever done for him—except give him his name and leave him his guitar?

But Ramie's new friends had assumed his personal quest; they had taken it on as their own. Chas was a knight in shining armor, promoting their causes like they were his own. Ramie wasn't sure he wanted that. Redfeather, his missing father, was Ramie's own private pain, a wound he licked, a scab he picked when no one was looking. Yet being with Chas and LaRoux was like nothing he had ever experienced. The quest for Redfeather was keeping them together, so he'd have to share it. He was willing to share it, but it scared him. Because what if they did find his father, what then?

Ramie had a scrap of a memory, an old recording deep in his brain that surfaced now and again like some old CD, all smudged and scratched. His father saying good-bye, explaining why he had to go away, how it wasn't his choice but he had to go. He couldn't recall the exact words, or even the quality of his voice. All he remembered was how he had felt to hear his father say good-bye and the great hole in his life that followed.

But what if his father had to run for his life? Maybe somebody was after him, wanted him dead; maybe he had to run from the law. Or maybe his mother had been a thorn in his heel, had driven him away with her nagging and harping. Ramie knew how demanding she could be. Maybe Redfeather had planned on returning for his son, once he made a name for himself. That's what his mother had said. She said his father had left the guitar because he wanted Ramie to remember him and think of him whenever he played it. *That way your father can always be with you, through the music.* Ramie had learned the chords; he could play a few songs. But he didn't feel in touch with his father when he played, not at all. It was a chore. He sounded lousy. Maybe he should practice more.

Part of the problem was that Ramie wasn't all that excited about the blues. That kind of music was way too mellow. He much preferred louder, faster music. Old-style heavy metal: thrashing, screaming, head-banging music. The classic metal was the best, the stuff from the eighties, created long before he was even born. That was the kind of music he identified with. Iron Maiden, Pantera, Megadeth—those great old bands best expressed the turmoil inside his soul. You can't shred like that on an acoustic guitar; you might as well try to play metal on a harp or a song flute.

A lot of kids his age were into rap, but the rhyming lyrics were kind of lame and the monotonous beat bored him. As for the blues, he had always thought it was old people's music—it all sounded pretty much the same. It was like country music—predictable chords, predictable lyrics. *Woe is me, my woman done left,* that kind of thing. But ever since hearing LaRoux, Ramie had a whole new appreciation for the blues.

Ramie's life was changing, and fast. He hadn't found his father yet, but if he had stayed in Cheyenne, he never would have met Chas or LaRoux. He would hang with them awhile longer; he wasn't ready to leave them. He couldn't wait to see what would happen next.

They lay in the grass feeling the warm on their backs, smelling the river, the mineral tang of mud, and a blend of other odors wafting by on a stir of June air. They were gypsies; they were a small, indigenous tribe. They were hobos waiting for an opportunity, a train to hop, a star to fall.

Cyclists and joggers passed by on the river path, not paying them any mind. They napped, sleeping like dogs on the grassy bank, arms and legs thrown wide. They woke with red stripes on their arms and faces where the sun had burned them. The three teens had nowhere to go, and they had not yet made a plan but were content to wait until hunger, thirst, or boredom drove them on.

Chas snapped off a dandelion by his ear and examined the yellow fibers, dusty with pollen, tasting them with his tongue.

"Did you know you can eat dandelions? You can make a healthy salad from the leaves. And wine, dandelion wine. You could survive a long time on dandelions."

Like you ever had to, Ramie thought, feeling irritable from the heat and wanting a shower. *You with your Visa debit card and your grandmother's car.* "Try living on crackers and ketchup soup from the condiment bar," he said. "You want to know how to survive on nothing, just watch me."

"Good idea," said Chas, ignoring Ramie's bitter tone. "Let's go on a raid, like the Apache used to do, like the border reivers of Scotland. Hit a lunch counter—a Panera or Einstein Bagel—grab us some saltines, sugar packs, and creamers. Or we can sneak-attack the free continental breakfasts some of the motels advertise." Chas had actually done this last week while passing through Illinois. "This time of year these motels are packed with travelers; they can't keep track of all the faces. They put out a spread every morning in the lobby, cafeteria style. Coffee, orange juice, bagels, bananas, hard-boiled eggs." He had lots of ideas of how to survive.

Driving downtown, looking for empty parking spaces with time left on them, Chas got lucky and slipped into one with over an hour left on the meter. "Like finding money!" he said triumphantly.

Ramie envied the way he handled the big Cadillac with ease. They walked across Civic Center Park, filled with transients sleeping under trees, and ended up inside the Denver Public Library, where it was air-conditioned. And where they could use the restrooms and drink from the water fountains. They had the Teen Zone to themselves. They sprawled on beanbag cushions and leafed through magazines while Chas recharged his phone.

"What are y'all going to do? When summer's over?"

"Jeez, LaRoux, summer just started." Ramie leafed through a new issue of *Guitar* magazine. He didn't want to think about the end of summer.

"Still, what are you going to do when you get back home?"

"I don't know. Get a job, I guess." Remembering his pending court date, he felt a wave of despair.

"What kind of job do you want?"

"A man job. But I'll probably end up flipping burgers for the summer."

"What's a man job?"

He tried to think of examples. "The oil fields. Heavy equipment operator. The military. When I turn eighteen, I'm going to enlist."

"But what about college? Aren't you going to college?"

Ramie snorted. "College is for people with money. Chas here, he's your frat boy." Ramie wore his poverty proudly, in a perverse way.

"Oh yeah, I'm rich, I'm rolling in it," Chas quipped, looking up from the screen. "I'm so loaded I'm camping out by the river with the homeless people."

"College isn't just for rich people, Ramie," LaRoux said, rolling onto her side on the beanbag, facing him square on through her dark bangs. "Maybe you can get a scholarship or go to night school. My brother goes to college and works at a pizza place."

"College is overrated," Chas said dismissively. "Anyway, you're going to be a singer, LaRoux. You're going to be famous. That's better than going to college."

"Singing is the only thing I can do. When I was in school, I got pulled out every day for special ed. I was one of *those* kids. 'Challenged.'" She made little quotation marks as she said it.

"All I know is you're the best damn singer I ever heard," Ramie said. "And you've got balls, girl! I mean, you've got what it takes. You're going to kick ass at the blues festival."

"He's right. You rule, LaRoux," said Chas. "You da bomb, babe."

LaRoux hugged her knees to her chest, savoring their praise. She had never felt so appreciated for being who she was. This was her real family; these were her spiritual brothers. Together they were the lost tribe of Israel, reunited.

Using his phone, Chas checked his bank balance online; it was down to eighty-nine dollars, and the Cadillac was a gas guzzler. "We need to raise a little cash before we hit the road," he informed his companions. "The question is, do we become beggars, buskers, or thieves?"

LaRoux twirled a strand of now-oily hair around her finger. "Um, what's a busker?"

"Like a performer. A street performer. That's what they called them in medieval days."

She snapped her fingers. "That's me. I want to be a busker! I like that word."

"OK, here's the plan. We divide and conquer. You and Ramie'll busk down on the Sixteenth Street Mall, singing and playing guitar. Meanwhile, I'm going to try my luck at being a street-corner entrepreneur."

LaRoux looked at him curiously. "A what?"

"A panhandler. A freeloader. A beggar. It must pay pretty good because there's somebody on every street corner in Denver, seems like. I'm going to make my own sign and give it a try. What's the worst that could happen?"

10

The next morning Chas installed LaRoux on the outdoor pedestrian mall at Sixteenth and Curtis and placed Ramie further down, at Welton. He seeded their guitar cases with the change gathered from his car, then, while they were tuning their guitars, Chas made himself a sign from a piece of cardboard from a Dumpster and a pen from LaRoux's backpack.

He left his cowboy hat in the trunk of the car. Cowboys didn't beg for money. Besides, the black hat was too hot to wear in the summer. It was definitely a winter hat. Maybe he should have bought a straw hat. This one had felt right in Cheyenne, but here in Denver it looked all wrong.

At Fourteenth and Broadway, across from the library, Chas paused and held up his sign to the oncoming traffic. When the light turned red and the cars stopped, that's when a driver might roll down the window and offer some money. It was mildly exciting, Chas discovered. Kind of like gambling. The odds weren't very good, but sometimes you got lucky. Or maybe it was skill. If you looked pathetic enough, or legitimate enough, like you deserved their help. You had to be convincing. Yet luck was involved, or fate, because some people driving by didn't have any money to give you, and some were so selfish and so filled with righteous entitlement they wouldn't give a dollar to a starving child. He wondered if there was a mathematical formula, some probability equation that would predict how long he would have to stand here, based on traffic flow maybe. Or…

Long minutes passed and he began to feel stupid. The light changed from green to yellow to red. Nobody rolled down the window. Most people looked away, not daring to make eye contact. The sun beat down. He was getting thirsty. Tired of standing. This was harder than he thought. He hoped Ramie and LaRoux were having better luck at street performing. This was a dumb idea, and he wished now he had gone with them.

His first hit was a silver-haired woman driving a Subaru Outback with two little kids in the back, strapped into car seats. She leaned out the window and gave him a dollar, followed by a bottle of water. "You're too young to be on the streets." She sounded like a schoolteacher. "Go to the Stout Street Clinic or the Salvation Army." The light turned green, the cars behind her honked their horns, and the Subaru sped off. One of the kids in the backseat waved to him.

Success! Chas was still pumped up about his first dollar when he saw a hard-worn old man hobbling toward him, an aluminum crutch under one arm. A handwritten sign hung from his neck.

VETERAN
Would work, except I can't, due to injury
Any amount will help
God bless America—and God bless you!

"Beat it, kid. This here is my corner."

"What do you mean, *your* corner?" Chas said, the anger rising. He had not expected this sort of treatment from a fellow panhandler.

"I don't know where you're from, but that's the way it works in this town. You stake out a claim, and this here is my territory. So git."

"I don't have to. It's a free country. I got my rights, same as you." Chas stepped aside for a tight-knit group of well-dressed Asians carrying umbrellas against the intense Colorado sun. The man with the crutch straightened his sign, but the tour guide said something in Japanese, probably a warning not to give the street people any money. As soon as they were out of earshot, the discussion continued.

"You don't have shit for rights, not on my corner, you don't. I don't tolerate interlopers—especially elite little shits like you! Now get on out of here."

"Elite? You called me elite?" Chas would not be bullied. He looked around for backup, but there was none. Cars flashed by and no one was paying the slightest bit of attention to two homeless people with signs, arguing. Chas was in his own little drama with this man. He felt for his knife, but didn't pull it out.

"OK, man, it's your street corner, I didn't know there were rules. But I'm not elite. You don't know what I've been through, you have no idea what my life is like."

"And I don't want to, I got troubles of my own. Call a cab, cream puff. I think I hear your mother calling you."

"Yeah? Well, why don't you try getting a job? I'll bet there's nothing wrong with your leg, and even if there is, there's places that hire handicaps. Have you even tried?"

The man swore at him and shook his crutch, but Chas took off, bolting across the street just before a rush of cars came at him. He walked fast, but he didn't look back. He walked with no destination in mind, heading east on Fourteenth Street for several blocks, his sign under one arm, carrying his water bottle in his free hand because it wouldn't fit in his pocket. His face burned; he was filled with rage. He wanted to kick something or punch somebody. Cars stopped at the light, but nobody rolled down the window of their air-conditioned cars. Nobody looked his way. Pedestrians crossed to the other side of the street to avoid him.

Chas was invisible. He was less than a pigeon; he was pigeon shit on the sidewalk. He walked another block and stopped, defeated. He couldn't even be a beggar; he had failed at that.

"Hot day, isn't it?" A thirtyish-looking man in snug designer jeans and metrosexual shoes handed Chas a folded bill. His matching French bulldogs strained at their retractable leashes, eager to continue their stroll.

Chas glanced at the bill—Alexander Hamilton—a tenner. Maybe there was a God. Filled with gratitude, he stuffed it into his front pocket and met the man's face. "Thanks!" He beamed, opening his heart to the kind stranger. "I appreciate this. You don't know how much it means to me. See, my mother back in Maryland, she's…I…" His voice went all squeaky. He took a deep breath and plunged on. "My mother's on life support, and they want to pull the plug. See, there are patients on the waiting list, people who could use her organs, and she's—"

"Save it, kid," the man interrupted, holding up his hand like he was stopping traffic. "I'm not interested. Keep the ten dollars. I don't care what you do with it; I don't want to know. But if you want my advice, lose the Evian bottle. It's a little too upscale." He winked and smiled. "For that matter, so are your shoes. Your average philanthropist wants the recipients of his generosity to look needy. No brand names. You've got to dress for success. The clothes make the man, but in your case, you want to dress down. Well, gotta go. The girls are straining at the leash. Toodles!" He took a step then turned to look over his shoulder at Chas. "Oh, and about your story? It's a bit over the top, don't you think? Keep it simple." Another mocking wink and Chas felt like he had been punched in the stomach.

"But it's true," he said. "About my mother."

The man was already moving on, crooning to his dogs; he was striding down the block in his metrosexual Jimmy Choo shoes, out of Chas's orbit, out of his life forever.

Chas threw his cardboard sign in the gutter and walked on. He had made twelve dollars in two hours, but he had taken a lot of abuse. He felt himself slow down, like the ground was sticky, like the lawn was drying cement. He realized he was lost.

Even though he knew the coordinates, the latitude and longitude because of the GPS on his phone, he did not know where he was going, or even where he wanted to go. He felt the planet was somehow revolving out of control beneath him, spinning at high speed. Got to keep moving, that's the thing. Keep moving, doesn't matter where. It's like freezing to death; once you stop moving, once you let the snow cover you, you're doomed. You become quite comfortable toward the end, they say. You become warm, or you think you're warm. And then you die. It's like going to sleep, he had read. But nobody knows what it's like to die.

His mother had stopped moving. She had gone to sleep, but she had not died. Not quite. Had she wanted to? Had she purposefully taken the pills with the vodka because she wanted to go to sleep and never wake up? Or had she been so drunk she took the pills without thinking? She was very forgetful, probably because she drank so much.

Chas had been the one to find her. He remembered feeling disgust at seeing her in a bra and panties sprawled across the unmade bed, a tangle of sheets that smelled like alcohol and urine.

"Mom! Wake up!" He grabbed her by the ankle and shook her foot, her dirty, calloused, uncared-for foot. "Mom!"

She didn't move, and fear flooded him like cold seawater. He felt to see if she was breathing, if she had a pulse, but he couldn't tell for sure. A string of saliva hung out of the side of her mouth. With shaking hands Chas had picked up the phone and called 9-1-1.

Chas was aware of his own heart beating. His head throbbed. He drank the last of the bottled water the Subaru lady had given him, but it wasn't nearly enough to quench his powerful thirst. It must have been ninety degrees. The sun was intense; he was sweating like a linebacker. Must keep moving, must find more water. Who could believe he could be this hot when he could see traces of snow on Mount Evans, to the west? Back home you couldn't see more than a few feet in front of you. Back home there were mountains, the Appalachian Mountains to the west of Frederick, but you couldn't see them, not from Reisterstown. The air was too hazy, maybe that was it. Out here the sky was clear, and you could see forever.

Chas came to a church, a massive stone church sheltered by lovely trees whose branches were welcoming arms swathed in green leaves. He went inside the wrought iron gate and tried to open the door to the sanctuary. Surely there would be a water fountain, a baptismal font, or at least a bathroom faucet inside. But the doors were locked, and no one answered his knock. Momentarily defeated, he sat down in the shade of one of the big trees, leaned against its rough hide, and gathered his resolve. It felt ten degrees cooler under this leafy umbrella. Nearby, two squirrels chased one another around the lawn before scampering up a neighboring tree, chattering in their secret squirrel language. Did the squirrels take any notice of him? They were all living parallel lives, existing in the same place in time yet mostly oblivious to each other. He thought of the birds in the trees and the ants busy in the ground beneath him, all going about their daily routines. They might as well be in different worlds, yet they were all connected without even knowing it.

Even now, fifteen hundred miles away, his mother still breathed, her heart still did its business; the many organs in her body were as busy as the ants, the squirrels, the birds. Except her brain. Her brain wasn't doing shit, they said. Her brain was dead.

Meanwhile, her favorite shows played day in and day out on the wall-mounted television opposite her bed. The nurses still turned her on schedule every two hours, watering her eyes with a squeeze bottle and swabbing her mouth with a little pink sponge on a stick, a sponge dipped in water. The nurses talked to her like she could hear them. Like she was an intelligent life form. But Mom never answered them. Nor did she respond to the little jabs from a safety pin on the bottoms of her feet—feet now scrubbed clean and the skin on her heels smoothed with Vaseline. Gran had even painted her toenails. She was like a life-sized doll to be dressed, groomed, and repositioned.

Meanwhile, people who could use her organs (not her much-abused liver but her undamaged ones—her kidneys, the size of fists; her pink heart, covered with nicks but resilient; her lovely corneas) were getting sicker. Blind people, people wasting away on dialysis, praying for miracles on their heart-lung machines. People who wanted to live. Maybe his mother wanted to live too but just didn't know how. Chas couldn't think about it right now, it was too much to bear. His life was closing in around him like a net; he had to keep moving. It was do or die, fight or flight.

11

On this June day, Denver's Sixteenth Street Mall was possibly the best place in the world to be homeless. The long, paved promenade of restaurants and stores was a pedestrian's carnival. Traffic was blocked except for the mall buses—you could ride them free of charge—and they drove by every few minutes, stopping at every intersection, all up and down Sixteenth Street. You could ride one of these buses all day long, if you wanted to—and a few homeless people did.

Chas had set Ramie and LaRoux up on separate blocks in hopes of bringing in more money. But no way was Ramie going to actually play his guitar out in the open, in front of all these people. As soon as Chas was out of sight, he had packed up his guitar and gone to find LaRoux. There she was, just a few blocks away, in front of a candle store, singing and playing her guitar like she was the half-time act at the Super Bowl. He joined her, tuning his guitar and strumming chords as best he could, accompanying her.

The tall buildings sheltered them from the high noon sun. The smell of the candles wafted out the door whenever a customer came out of the shop. More tantalizing were the food smells—fried onions and exotic spices—which piqued Ramie's appetite to the point of exquisite pain. His belly roared with hunger, but playing chords helped take his mind off of food. Drenched in LaRoux's voice, he concentrated on playing as well as he was able and faking it when he wasn't sure.

LaRoux sang like she was on a mission. Her face lit up, her body twitched; it was a thing to behold. She gave herself over to the song; she was a tool of the music, jerking and tossing her black hair. Quite a few people turned their heads to look as they passed. Some even stopped long enough to nod their heads, smile their approval, and toss a handful of coins into the open guitar case. Occasionally a dollar bill dropped, fluttering like a butterfly.

Ramie was content to be there for her. He was more than content—he was fulfilled to be whatever she needed: a backup rhythm man, a bodyguard, a roadie, a friend, a boyfriend. He was happy watching her head jerk and her hair flip and toss. He was amazed to be here, right here on the Sixteenth Street Mall in Denver, Colorado, strumming chords while LaRoux sang to the strangers passing by, making up words and sounds, putting them together in a brand new way.

A young man in a shirt and tie, jacket slung over his arm, reached in his pocket and dropped a ten-dollar bill into the open guitar case.

LaRoux followed him with her eyes.

They took a break; LaRoux was dying of thirst, her voice was getting all raspy. Ramie loped down to Subway where he asked if he could have a cup of water, and to his amazement, the girl behind the counter gave him a cup and said, "There's the machine, help yourself. The little silver lever next to the Sprite, that's the water." The world was good; people were generous and caring. He wondered if LaRoux would rather have ice tea instead, but he hadn't paid for ice tea. He had asked for water, and the girl behind the counter had trusted him to fill the cup with water. It was a matter of honor.

Ramie quenched his own thirst, then filled the cup with ice and water for LaRoux, carrying it back to her, feeling amply rewarded as he watched her guzzle it down.

After they had collected a few more coins, Ramie and LaRoux packed up their guitars and rode the bus up and down Sixteenth Street, getting off at Twist and Shout to look at CDs and movies, then over to Hard Rock Café for a basket of french fries.

"Someday your autographed guitar might be on these walls," he said, loving the dreamy look that came over her face.

"What about you, Ramie? Don't you want to be a musician too?" She reached for a hot, salty french fry.

"I'm not that good yet." He dropped his head shyly, copper coils of hair dropping in front of his eyes. "But I want to be." LaRoux brushed his hair aside, and he shivered at the touch of her fingers against his forehead.

"You are good. You are so much better than you know, Ramie Redfeather."

His heart did a cartwheel followed by a backflip with a half twist. She liked him! He knew it, he could feel it.

Without Chas here, it was different. Chas was the catalyst; Chas brought out something in each of them that otherwise went undiscovered. Without Chas they never would have met. Still, Ramie was awfully glad Chas wasn't here right now to spoil this moment.

They went back to the candle store, tuned their guitars, and started again, renewed. LaRoux's exuberance was something to behold. Slowly the quarters accumulated, along with a scattering of one-dollar bills. Her voice got all and hoarse, and Ramie loved it all the more. His fingers were sore. He wasn't used to playing more than a few chords at a time. Maybe they would start bleeding. He hoped they would.

"I'm Lozen LaRoux, and we're looking for Redfeather," she said to the strangers passing by. "This song is for him. If anybody knows where he's at, we'd appreciate it if you'd give us a clue." She launched into another song Ramie didn't know but could follow because it was the same chord progression, the same basic song as so many others, yet as unique as a fingerprint, a face, a human heart.

Ramie thought again about what he would say to the man—if he ever found him. He imagined the scenario, tried out his opening line. *Ray Redfeather? That's my name too. I go by Ramie. Do you remember me? I'm your son.*

He had no idea what his father looked like, but he had formed a mental image based on a photograph of Naiche, son of Cochise, a photo he had seen online somewhere. Naiche, sometimes called Natchez, was a handsome man. Ramie imagined his father to have the same straight nose, the same penetrating gaze. Naiche's mouth resembled Ramie's own, or so he thought, with the little crease above the full upper lip. Not smiling, but not scowling either. A handsome face; a face full of life.

Ramie's earliest memory was looking out the school bus window and waving to his mother. It must've been the first day of kindergarten. He pressed his face against the glass, his heart catching on something sharp. She was smiling and crying at the same time, reminding him of a rainbow, the sun shining through the rain. *Why is she crying?* he had wondered. *Is school a very bad place?* He must've been, what, five years old?

His father had been long gone by then. But he soon had a baby brother and a puppy of his own to take care of. Brandon and Boogie.

Wait—how old was he when Boogie got run over by a car and had to be put down? Seven or eight? No, he had to have been older than that. He had to have been nine, at least. The human mind was not very reliable, not when it came to keeping an accurate record of things. Computers were much better. Yet he did remember. He remembered very clearly his mother carrying the dog to the car with a towel wrapped around what was left of his hind leg. His mother's face was savage.

It was winter, bitter Wyoming cold, and she had chipped the ice off the windshield so furiously she broke the plastic scraper and threw it across the yard, cursing. Ramie sat shivering in the back seat, Boogie's head in his lap, the dog's pale tongue showing as he panted, looking to Ramie with his trusting eyes. The memory hurt; it caused a squeezing pain in his chest to remember it. He had watched his dog die. He had held him, stroked his ears for the last time as the vet drew up the syringe. "Boogie will be out of his misery, he'll be at peace. Say good-bye." He had imagined that Boogie would relax after the shot and drift off to sleep, dreaming those dog dreams, and then gradually his breathing would slow and his heart would stop. Instead, the syringe of poison was like an instant death ray. The vet pushed the plunger, Boogie flinched, and seconds later he was dead. Completely and utterly dead. Ramie shed a tear for his dear childhood friend.

For the first time, he wondered how his mother had managed to pay for it—an off-hours visit to have Boogie put out of his misery. It must've cost a lot of money. Money they didn't have. They were poor; he had begun to realize that after his dog died. Poorer than most of his friends. He hated being poor. Being a waitress was a suck-ass job, he decided. He would never wait tables, no sir. He, Ramie, was going to make a lot of money when he got out of school. He'd give his mother enough so she could quit that restaurant, give her enough so she could retire and raise rescued dogs. She loved dogs—she loved how they needed her, how they adored her. They were far more obedient than he and Brandon were.

After Boogie she took in more dogs, but she could never afford to take care of them properly—all the shots they needed, all the good quality food they were supposed to have. Ramie's own immunizations were from the clinic, but even then they weren't entirely free, and he wasn't sure he had ever received all the shots he was supposed to. His mother never said much about his father. A person should have some memory of the man who fathered him. Or at least a photograph, an anecdote, something to hold onto. His mother didn't have much to offer, other than the guitar. *This was your father's; he wanted you to have it. Maybe you've inherited his talent for music. That man could sure play a guitar. His hands, his voice—he could've been a star. You take that guitar, son, and you learn to play it. You do him proud, and you do me proud, Ramie.*

She bought him guitar lessons. He was only ten, but his hands were big for his age. Big enough to wrap around the neck and press down on the strings. He went to the music store for private instruction every Saturday morning for six weeks—and then suddenly his mother couldn't afford it anymore. It had been a start. He could play some chords; he could pick out a simple melody. Now, here on Denver's Sixteenth Street Mall with LaRoux, Ramie wished he had practiced a whole lot more. He'd just have to make up for lost time. Maybe he could play with LaRoux in the contest down in Austin. Maybe.

It was late in the afternoon when Chas met up with Ramie and LaRoux on the mall. He was carrying two plastic bags.

"Looks like you struck it rich. Two whole bags of money?"

"Not. Panhandling is a dangerous sport. I was nearly killed by the street corner cartel," Chas explained as he handed out warm and squishy Burrito Supremes, redolent of cheese and hot sauce. "It was happy hour at Taco Bell. I got twelve bean and cheese burritos for six dollars and change."

"Is that how much you made?" LaRoux didn't think that sounded like very much money.

"Ha! I made a hundred bucks," he gloated.

"You made a hundred dollars standing on the street corner holding a stupid sign?" said Ramie, astonished.

"Hell, no. Begging nearly got me killed. I got smart. Took the GPS out of the car and sold it for cash."

"You sold your granny's GPS? You are a piece of work, Chas."

"Won't you need it? To find your way back home?" LaRoux asked."

"Don't worry, darlin', I've got an app on my iPhone. Besides, I'm not going back anytime soon. I think we ought to take this show on the road. Call it LaRoux's World Tour."

"Yeah, like Iron Maiden's tour, *Flight 666*," Ramie said excitedly. "Bruce Dickinson flew the Ed Force One around the world in forty-five days, playing in thirteen countries. Out of the way places, like India and Peru and Ecuador. I was hoping like hell they would fly into Cheyenne, but they didn't."

"Instead of a Boeing 757, I'll drive us in a 1960 Cadillac Eldorado," said Chas. "And we'll play Cheyenne, baby, I promise you."

They sat leaning against the wall, red sauce dripping onto their T-shirts as they devoured the burritos and made outrageous plans, scarcely noticing the passersby who were but stagehands and stand-ins in their grand performance. *This is it*, thought Chas. *Right here, right now, my life*.

"What's in the other bag?" Ramie asked.

"Oh, that? It's your new gig, bro. From Colorado Memories."

"Huh?"

"Colorado Memories. A souvenir store. Classic kitsch with a Western theme."

"Why do I get the feeling I'm not going to like this?"

"Are you kidding me? You're not going to like this, you're going to love it." He flashed his perfected Chas grin as he reached into the bag and pulled out an imitation Indian headdress.

Ramie groaned. "Tell me this is a joke."

"No joke." Chas pulled out a plastic bow-and-arrow set, a plastic quiver, and a red vinyl breechcloth, laying them on the sidewalk at Ramie's feet. "You're a walking gold mine, my red friend. This will help you reconnect with your inner Apache."

"What makes you think I'm actually going to wear this made-in-China piece of shit? Why don't you wear it?"

"Because you're the Indian"

"Man, this is just wrong."

"Why is it wrong? This is your big moment. Your chance to commune with your ancestors and make us some money."

"Dude, those are, like, chicken feathers. A plastic fucking tomahawk? You bought it, you wear it. I can't believe you spent money on that."

"OK, so it's not authentic, so what? It was on sale, half price. We'll make our money back in twenty minutes, guaranteed."

"People will think—"

"People won't think shit, what do they know? You put the costume on with pride. LaRoux paints your face with her blue nail polish, and you dance around, shaking these." He produced some plastic Mexican maracas from deep within the bag.

LaRoux licked a dollop of sour cream out of the taco bag with her long, pink tongue. "Yeah, Ramie. It's time somebody else did some singing. My voice needs a break." She smiled craftily. "You'll do it for me, won't you?"

"What about moccasins?" Ramie asked sullenly.

"Moccasins, are you kidding me? We can't afford moccasins. You can dance in your bare feet. Bare chest and bare feet—it'll be way more authentic."

"You want me to take my shirt off too?"

"Duh! Have you ever seen an Indian wearing a Cannibal Corpse T-shirt?"

"Yeah, me. I'm an Indian, and I'm wearing it."

Chas shook his head impatiently. "That doesn't count."

"That doesn't count?"

"You know what I mean. You can't play an Indian wearing a death metal T-shirt. It's not genuine. People want authenticity."

LaRoux laughed. "I agree with Chas. You might be half Apache, Ramie. But you can't play an Indian in those clothes. Strip down, boy. Off with that shirt, show me your man nipples. Come on, it'll be fun!"

"Easy for you to say. Nobody's asking you to take your shirt off."

"Hey, bro," Chas said, "if you need a little firewater for fortification, that can be arranged. How about a nice Muscadet from the Loire Valley?"

Ramie scowled, but it was only for effect. He knew he was going to do it, it was just a matter of sticking to his principles.

"I'll even chill it for you." Chas rattled the ice in his supersized to-go cup.

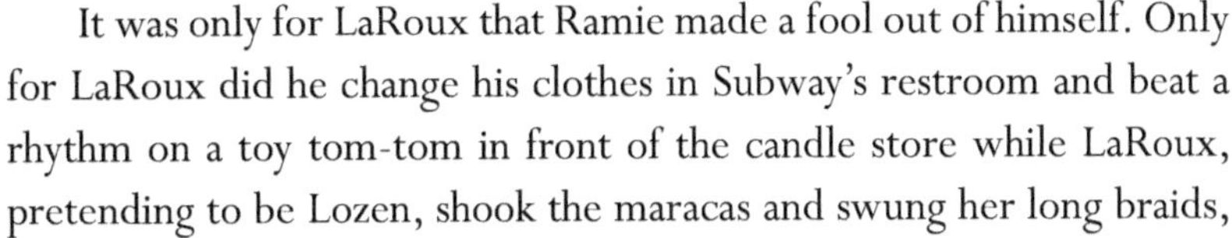

It was only for LaRoux that Ramie made a fool out of himself. Only for LaRoux did he change his clothes in Subway's restroom and beat a rhythm on a toy tom-tom in front of the candle store while LaRoux, pretending to be Lozen, shook the maracas and swung her long braids, even though Chas said Apache women didn't plait their hair. Not that he was a stickler for authenticity; for him it was more the effect, the emotional truth.

By five o'clock they had made eighteen dollars and forty-five cents.

Is this really worth it? Chas wondered. Maybe they should just get in the car and go, as fast as possible, in the direction of Austin, Texas. Just drive like the wind.

12

They stood just inside the doorway, hesitant, blinking, their eyes adjusting to the drastic change in light.

A blues bar is a pretty sad place at two o'clock in the afternoon, LaRoux decided. A dark, sour-smelling cave of a place. A fat man sat at the bar, overflowing his stool. His big hand wrapped around a glass, he stared blankly at a baseball game on the flat screen. Across the room, some guy played a video game, half-empty bottle beside him.

"Help you?" an old man behind the bar asked. Gray hair, black skin creased like a raisin.

"We're looking for Redfeather," Chas said. Chas, the spokesperson.

"Is that a fact? And who might you be?"

"We're new in town. Miss LaRoux here, she's a musician from Baton Rouge."

"Pleased to meet you." He continued to wipe down the bar.

"We heard Redfeather's in Denver."

The bartender glanced at his watch. "That may be, but wherever he is, I suspect he is still sleeping at this hour." A soft laugh. "I just opened my doors, and the music don't start until later tonight. Usually about nine."

"Is he scheduled to play here anytime soon?"

The man shook his head. "He ain't played here in years. But if you find him, tell him old Jim Spate would sure like to see him again."

"So you know him?" Ramie spoke up at last. "You actually know Redfeather?"

"Sure, I know him," the black man chuckled. "Lots of people knows him. What you want with him?

Ramie was struck dumb, mute as a stone. LaRoux cleared her throat and looked at him. *Why* are *we looking for Redfeather?* she wondered.

"Actually, we're looking to jam with him," Chas said. "We heard he's good." He put his hand on the singer's shoulder. "Miss LaRoux here, she's a singer, and Ramie here, he's her backup."

"And who are you?

"I'm their manager."

"Shoot, I must be getting old," the bartender said, scratching his head. "You all look like teenagers to me."

"Well, you have to start young if you want to make it in this business."

Jim Spate's laugh was dry, and caused him to go into a coughing jag. "You start too young, you're all wrung out at twenty-five," he finally managed to say. "A downhill slide from there. I need a drink. You kids want a Coke or something? Ice tea?"

The bar was dark and cool, and the three were reluctant to leave, unsure of where they would go next. "A Coke would be just the thing," said Chas, sitting down on a barstool.

Ramie nodded, joining him.

"Ice tea, please." LaRoux climbed up on a stool, her feet dangling. "Sweet."

The bartender brought them their drinks.

"Redfeather, he's a good bluesman, he's a mean guitar player. I heard rumors he was staging a comeback here in Denver."

Ramie felt a flush of pride at that. To stage a comeback you have to have been somebody to begin with.

"But I ain't seen him in a long time. I figured he went back home," the old man added, reconsidering.

"Home?" Ramie said, thinking of Cheyenne. "Where's that?"

"I can't say, exactly. The Rez, I reckon. He had people down there."

The kids talked at once, pelting him with questions.

"Down where?"

"Which reservation?"

"Who are his people?"

Old Jim laughed, raising his arms as if to fend off the barrage. "Don't know if he ever said, and if he did, I don't remember. My knowledge of Redfeather is of a different nature, and my memory for other stuff ain't so good these days. Worse 'n my eyesight. But you kids sure you're not the junior league of private detectives or something? Why you all so interested in Redfeather?"

LaRoux decided to look after her own interests. "Actually, I'm looking for a gig. Redfeather, he's…" She twirled a strand of hair, groping for words.

"An inspiration," Chas finished smoothly, swirling his glass of Coke like it was a complex Bordeaux. "A huge influence on her. On all of us."

The bartender looked from one to another, bemused. "So where you kids from? And how you know about Redfeather?"

Chas looked to Ramie who flushed and dropped his head. He really didn't know anything about Redfeather, except that he had been named after him.

No one spoke. A crowd's roar from the televised baseball game. The electronic noises from the video game. Chas rushed to fill the void.

"Mae B. LaRoux here, she's awesome, you should hear her sing. Are you looking for new talent?"

The man now smiled wide enough to show the gap in his yellow teeth. "I'm always lookin' for talent. You got a demo, Miss LaRoux?"

She looked down at her hands in her lap, embarrassed. She didn't know how to do that. Make a demo. It probably cost money—more than she had.

"She played Ziggies," Ramie offered.

"And a couple of venues in Kansas City," Chas added. "She's playing in Texas next week. At the blues festival."

"I'm hoping to make a little cash before we head down there."

Old Jim laughed. "Me too, sugar. I'm always lookin' to make a little cash. That's the life of a musician, ain't it?" He set his towel down, came out from behind the bar, and picked up a guitar from a rack on the wall, a wall filled with photos, most of them signed, probably famous musicians and other famous personalities. Old Jim pulled out a stool and played a chord then paused to tune the strings. He played the chord again.

"We're all looking to make a little cash to tide us over." The old bluesman tightened the D string and plucked it again. "What you want at your stage of the game are open mike nights, jam sessions, that sort of thing. There's an open mike night every Wednesday at Bushwackers, that would be a good place to start. See, you gotta work your way in, prove yourself, pay your dues. Make some friends along the way. Then, if you get lucky, you make a name for yourself. Can't be impatient; it don't work that way. It's a lifestyle, music is. It's a road. A long road, and it's bumpy and washed out in places. But it's the only road I know."

He continued to tune the guitar, staring up at the ceiling, having no need of his eyes, which they could now see looked crystallized, like marbles, like golden-brown tiger's eyes. Satisfied with the sound, he launched into a little riff, his gnarled fingers moving easily over the strings. The music was sad, and it resonated in them, it felt familiar. In sixty seconds he had summarized the emotions of their lives.

"Now then, tell me why you all are really looking for Redfeather."

LaRoux looked hopefully toward Ramie, but he stood with his hands in his pockets, staring at his shoes.

"He's Ramie's father," Chas said, wondering with irritation why it was Ramie never spoke for himself.

"I wish you wouldn't tell people that," Ramie snapped, his cheeks burning. "He might be my father. I think he's my father, but I don't know for sure."

"Oh, I see. You're on a father quest. I got to tell you, they don't usually go well."

"Hey, Jim, can I get another beer here?" the guy at the video game called out.

"There's usually a reason folks run off," the old man said, looking at Ramie. "Sometimes a man gotta be his own father, in a way of speaking. Got to reinvent a whole new line, raise himself, find himself, make himself a new family. Know what I mean?"

Settling into his chair, the musician played another lick, his crooked, bitten-down fingers right at home on the frets. He crooned along, a wordless phrase that sounded like somebody sobbing.

Jim Spate paused, scrutinizing them with his old tiger's eyes as if he were reading their futures.

"Well, don't just stand there with your lips hanging low. Go get your guitars, let's play us a little afternoon blues."

13

At a late-night coffee shop on Colfax the three teens sprawled on sagging, comfortable couches, sharing a large double latte between them. They sipped it slowly, making it last. The satellite radio played the My Chemical Romance song about teenagers, and it somehow fit their collective mood. They were in no great hurry to spread their sleeping bags on the banks of the Platte; it was way too early for that.

Chas was taking advantage of the free Wi-Fi, catching up on his Internet social life. Ramie leafed through a ragged issue of *Spin*, coffee-stained, pages ripped out. He came across an article, an interview with Dave Mustaine. Ramie had been told that he looked like the Megadeth guitarist (well, actually he had been told that his *hair* looked like Mustaine's hair), and this pleased Ramie. If he couldn't play guitar like Mustaine, at least he could remind people of Megadeth. Ramie wasn't the kind of person who had to be the center of attention, the front man, the celebrity. He was more of a team player. If only he had a team.

LaRoux flipped through the pages of a two-month-old *People* magazine, skimming over the photos while studying her new friends. Chas held the world in the palm of his hand, doing his Chas thing, absorbing information as fast as his thumbs brought it to the screen. She envied Chas's mind, how he seemed to breathe in whole paragraphs at a glance. And Ramie too; Ramie was smart, maybe even as smart as Chas, though he preferred not to show it off. Ramie was smart in a different way, a slower way. A deeper way. Not to mention, he was exotic. That tangled mane of copper-colored hair hanging over his Apache cheekbones, his dark eyes—the combination was totally unexpected. And alluring.

Ramie and Chas were both one of a kind, each in his own way. She too was one of a kind, but life would be much easier if her brain worked like other people's brains. Her parents had never taken her back to that doctor—what was his name? She wished she could remember his name. Instead, they had found another school, a Christian academy, and when that didn't work out they found a charter school with really mean teachers who didn't know anything about syndromes and learning differences. "It's a good thing she's pretty," her father had said to her mother on numerous occasions, as if LaRoux hadn't been standing there.

At 10:30 p.m. Chas texted his grandmother—a time when he knew she would be asleep and he wouldn't have to deal with an angry response or a call back right away. For the first week after what they referred to as "the accident," she kept her phone on all the time, within arm's reach, in case the hospital should call. But it wore her out, she said, waiting for the phone to ring every minute of the day, it was mentally exhausting.

Gran announced she would no longer be available twenty-four hours a day. She had to start looking after herself. She now turned her phone off every night when she went to bed. If her daughter died during the wee hours, the nurses could reach her after eight o'clock the next morning, after she had had her first cup of coffee. Gran had been dealing with his mom her whole life, and it was wearing her out.

Hi Gran, it's me, he texted. *Everything is OK*. (He had to spell every-thing out for Gran; she wasn't adept in the shorthand of texting. It took a lot longer, but he had to be explicit; he needed her compliance.)

I'm in Denver, Colorado, the mile-hi city! There are a couple of schools I want to see. I've got interviews at D.U. (which was a fib) *and C.U.* (also a fib). *Good schools, both! I know you are upset with me but I hope you'll forgive me, I m taking real good care of George's car and you'll be proud of me one of these days when I m a doctor, physicist, etc.* He thought about asking about his mother, but he couldn't bring himself to type the words.

LaRoux felt a sudden need to be back home where there was always a pitcher of sweet tea in the fridge, where the television was always on (even when no one was in the room, because her mother couldn't stand the sound of silence; it made her feel lonely), and where she had her very own bathroom with a shower and bathtub. She hadn't had a shower for days, had been taking bird baths in public restrooms.

She was missing old Riley, good old Riley left behind when Luke went away to college and now abandoned by her as well. She pictured him lying on his doggy bed with Monkey, his rag doll, ears lifting when he heard the rattle of the key in the lock. Her eyes stung, remembering the way he cocked his head to one side when you talked to him, the feel of his wet nose against her face. The way he wiggled and barked when-ever she said, "Where's the monkey? Where's the monkey? Go get the monkey!" She thought about calling home on Chas's phone just to speak to Riley, to reassure him she was all right. But not yet. The number would show on the caller ID, and Daddy would see it; he was real smart, he would suspect something. So she had to wait until Austin, after the contest, after she was a winner. Then what could they say? She would go home then, for a while. But as an adult—as Lozen LaRoux. Or maybe Austin LaRoux. She kind of liked the sound of that. A name that would forever remind her of her musical breakout.

She watched Chas texting, wondering if he was texting one of his friends back home. Or was he texting his grandmother, maybe asking her to put some money in his account? Chas seemed close to his grandmother. LaRoux wished she had a grandparent she was close to. Grandma Mary had dementia; she had been put into a nursing home. Every time LaRoux went to visit her, the old lady accused her of stealing her purse. The other grandparents, Gigi Ellen and Pops Joe, were always traveling, doing God's work in faraway places whose names she couldn't pronounce.

"Is your gran still mad at you?" she asked Chas.

He shrugged. "She'll get over it."

"So what about your mom?" LaRoux asked Ramie, whose long body was sprawled on an easy chair, one leg dangling over the worn-out arm. "Will she call the cops?"

Ramie looked up from the magazine and shook a coil of hair out of his face. "She doesn't need any more trouble than she's already got. I got a court date coming up."

"A court date? What for?"

"Murder one."

"Tell me you're kidding."

"Duh! Do I look like a killer?"

"I don't know," said LaRoux. "What's a killer look like?"

He shook his head, bared his teeth, and crossed his eyes. The jagged little bark that was LaRoux's laugh snagged his heart.

"Come on, Ramie," Chas said. "Tell us. What did you do?"

Ramie hated being put on the spot. "I didn't steal a car," he quipped. "Like some people I know."

"Yeah? You don't seem to have any qualms riding around in it. So what did you steal?"

Remembering the incident, and the rage that had provoked it, made Ramie feel a little queasy. Brandon was being made fun of, mocked for the way he talked. It had been going on for some time, though his little brother was too ashamed to tell anybody. When Ramie had found out, he wanted to punch the kid's face; he wanted to seriously injure him, a kid named Hunter, he had found out. It was Hunter who left a message on their phone, imitating Brandon's speech impediment, pretending to solicit money for the mentally retarded. It hurt Ramie worse than if he was the one being ridiculed. It had been going on for some time Brandon admitted when Ramie confronted him. Brandon did talk through his nose; it was called "velopharyngeal insufficiency," a medical term that sounded better than "talks like a retard." His brother had been born with the defect, which could be fixed surgically, but the operation wasn't covered by their insurance. The surgery cost almost as much as his mother made in a year.

Ramie couldn't bear it. He couldn't beat Hunter's face as he deserved—the punk was only eleven years old, and he was afraid he'd kill him. So he'd cased their house and broken in when no one was home, taking a baseball bat to everything in Hunter's bedroom—his TV, his computer, his PlayStation, his games—smashing the living shit out of them, and writing THIS IS YOUR FACE, HUNTER on the wall with a Magic Marker, then signing his name, Ramie Redfeather, big and bold as John Hancock. As he was swinging the bat, he had felt the satisfaction of revenge, but soon after the pain seeped back into his heart and turned bitter.

"I didn't steal anything," he told his friends. "I'm charged with breaking and entering," he told his friends, "and willful destruction of property."

Chas saw the look on his face and decided not to question him further. Ramie was not one to talk much, Chas had discovered. The strong, silent type. Chas was glad to have Ramie on his side because he would be a formidable enemy.

"I hope you don't get the hangin' judge, my friend."

"Chas, can I borrow your phone?" LaRoux wanted to text her friend Jordan to make sure she was still texting LaRoux's parents every day, like she had promised she would.

Hi how r u? All ok @ camp? My mom cool?

Ya, but u should b here! OMG Some hot Sr. counselor babes, u r missing out!

Of course, Jordan was in love; Jordan was always in love. Her friend was one of those golden girls with sleek, smooth, honey-colored hair—highlighted with chunks of blonde. She had even-toned skin that looked like plastic and big white teeth like piano keys. Jordan was shapely; Jordan was popular, with adults as well as her peers. Adults liked her because she knew how to talk to them, how to answer their questions; she told them what they wanted to hear with a toothy smile.

But LaRoux had something on Jordan, and Jordan would cover for her, not because she was all that loyal to her friend from church but because LaRoux knew that Jordan had a tattoo on her back. Actually, it was just above the crack of her butt cheeks, peeking over the elastic of her skimpy panties. And it was not a cute little butterfly. It was not a rose or a green shamrock either. No sir. Jordan had a tattoo of a round, red apple with a bite out of it and BITE ME! written over it, like an invitation. The inked design was about the size of her open hand, a tramp stamp if there ever was one, and was definitely not something Jordan wanted Daddy and Mommy to ever find out about.

LaRoux texted Jordan back. *Miss u bestie! IOU! Give mom and dad my luv. lmfao!*

The three began to grow heavy-eyed, and fighting it off, they went out into the Denver night. The air felt like silk against their bare arms. They walked Colfax under the yellow streetlights, watching the people, the underworld people, going about their night business, thrilling to see. Chas was looking to buy some weed, a few hits of acid, a little E, some mushrooms—anything to heighten the experience—but his father had taught him never to buy from strangers. It could be a setup. You could get arrested, robbed, you could get killed. And with strangers there was no quality control. You usually got fucked.

Luckily, Colorado had relaxed rules about selling medicinal and recreational marijuana; there were telltale green crosses on nearly every block. The bell above the door tinkled as they went inside, like a general store from yesteryear, and the slightly musty smell filled their heads. It reminded LaRoux of a teahouse—the smell and the way the dried leaves were displayed in bins behind glass, to be scooped out, weighed, and packaged up. There was a wide assortment of smoking devices, vaporizers, pipes of all shapes and sizes—all different, with as much personality as tea sets and cozies, she thought. The smell, that was what she liked best. The burning sweetness hanging in the air, then gone. And the sense of sharing, of passing the joint, the pipe, from hand to hand, from mouth to mouth. It was like a secret ceremony, a pledge among friends. Hadn't the Indians passed the peace pipe?

What she didn't like was the rawness in her throat and the tightness in her chest when she held the smoke inside. When it was her turn to take a puff—a hit, a toke—she put her lips to it, feeling the warmth of other lips and of the fire so close to her mouth. She just pretended to suck in, then passed it on, watching the others get all relaxed and red-eyed.

They talked about heading south. Chas had Googled *Apache reservation* and found there were actually four designated tribal lands in New Mexico and Arizona, and several more in Texas. Chas was becoming an Apache expert; he quoted Victorio, Cochise, Santana, and Geronimo. *Once I moved with the wind.* But he was not the only one who researched the Indians.

LaRoux had taken a book from the Denver Public Library. She'd put it in her pack and walked right out the door with it, half expecting an alarm to sound, but none did. The book was called *Warrior Woman: The Story of Lozen, Apache Warrior and Shaman.* She knew it would take her a long time to read it, but it seemed like the most important book in her life. Just holding it in her hands made her feel connected to the real Lozen, whose hands were the instruments through which Ussen's power worked. Ussen, she had read, was the Apache name for the Creator of everything – the same Creator who had given LaRoux her voice. She felt bad now for stealing the book.

14

For the next few days, they rose early in their camp, along the South Platte, and washed their faces in the river before going to work as buskers on the Sixteenth Street Mall. Breakfast was a Kit Kat or a package of Ho Hos and a cup of coffee. Starbucks was now beyond their means; instead, they bought pint-sized coffee at 7-Eleven, stirring in several thimble-size cartons of half-and-half and as much sugar as would dissolve. Lunch was a hot dog from Oscar's cart; he gave them a special price on the all-beef franks. They spent nearly every quarter they made on food and drinks, and at the end of the day they had little to show other than sore feet and sunburned faces.

They became aware of the marginal people. The transients, like them. People on the move, tramping across town carrying all they owned on their back, lining up at the homeless shelters for free food. At night some of them constructed temporary little camps along the river. All of these people, like city pigeons, living in the eaves and between the cracks, picking up society's crumbs. And like the pigeons, just as despised, those dirty birds.

After performing all day for spare change, Chas drove to a gas station where they slipped into the restroom to brush their teeth and bathe in the sink, using pink hand soap from a dispenser and rough brown paper towels. Gas stations were better than fast food restaurants or convenience stores for this purpose; they weren't monitored as closely. Nobody much cared what you did in a gas station restroom. They gave you the key on a great big stick, and you took it back when you were finished. No questions asked.

Back at camp they made their own version of happy hour, Ramie busting out the crackers and ketchup, Chas chilling a bottle of wine in the river while LaRoux soaked her feet. They sprawled on a grassy spot along the sloping bank, strangely content, LaRoux's head resting on Ramie's stomach, her feet on Chas's, like the letter H. They napped like cats in the late afternoon sun.

Cyclists, joggers, and skaters sped by on the bicycle path that followed the river on its course from the mountains, through the city, and north through the industrial part of Denver. These were healthy-looking people with money enough to buy the right shoes, the right gear; they were using the path to stay in shape, to train, to enjoy the out-of-doors. Then along came a gray-haired woman wearing a tattered green cocktail dress and cheap running shoes. She was pushing a grocery cart heaped with who knows what, all tied down under a blue plastic tarp. Singing, "The ants come marching one by one, hurrah, hurrah."

I'm like her, LaRoux thought. *She is me; I am her, or could be.* Although LaRoux technically had a home, if she wanted to return. Her parents would surely take her back, but there would be a price to pay. She would have to atone.

The river slid by, chortling in spots where the eddies formed, carrying leaves, twigs, cans, and Styrofoam cups out of the city, toward the Great Plains. Toward the Mississippi. Toward the Gulf Coast. LaRoux was from Baton Rouge, Chas thought, with a little shiver of wonder. To think that the water flowing by them this moment would pass by her hometown in, what, a couple of weeks? How long would it take a molecule of water to travel that journey? But LaRoux didn't want to talk about Baton Rouge. She was so done with her past life. Except for a few little things she missed, like her mother's ice tea. And beignets; nobody out here knew what a beignet was. After church on Sundays, her father always stopped at Café Beignet for a dozen of the fresh, warm, squishy pillows of fried dough that left a telltale ring of sugar around your mouth and a little sticky spot on the tip of your nose. They took them home and ate them around the kitchen table. Church and beignets were a Sunday ritual for the Appleby family. But she didn't want to think about her past life.

LaRoux's tiny fingers combed and twisted the locks of Ramie's extraordinary hair, weaving colored beads into the thin braids she was making. She hummed as she braided, the contented buzz of a honeybee.

"Well now, don't you look just like Captain Jack Sparrow," sniped Chas, rolling onto his side and plucking a blade of flattened grass to chew on.

Ramie was ecstatic, feeling LaRoux's hands in his hair. Sometimes it hurt as she pulled tightly in her skillful girl knowledge of hair and beads. One tug nearly brought tears to his eyes, yet he wanted her never to stop. He pictured the two of them, naked in the sun, her hair and his entwined, her small breasts uncovered for him to see, but the fantasy was interrupted by the pain of his hair being pulled hard.

"Ow! What are you doing?"

"Hold still and quit whining." LaRoux was all business. She was as intent as a baboon picking lice from a baby's hide. "And now for the finishing touch. You won't believe what I found under that tree." She pulled a feather out of her pocket. A black feather with a red tip. "Isn't it awesome?" She wrapped a piece of tooth floss around the quill and wove it among the hair and beads where it hung just below his left ear.

"There you are, Ramie. Ramie Redfeather. Doesn't it suit him, Chas? Isn't he so original?"

"Yeah, whatever."

LaRoux felt a pang of sympathy for Chas. He was jealous, jealous of her attentions. Imagine! She had never felt so wanted. Two boys who liked her at the very same time. This never would have happened back home in Baton Rouge.

"Come over here, Chas. Sit down, I've got something to make for you. I've been saving these beads, these leather strips. This is going to be for you."

"What is it?"

"It's going to be a—a—like a necklace. A lariat, I guess you'd call it. To go with your cowboy hat."

Chas was somewhat mollified. "How'd you learn that?

"How did I learn what? Braiding or beading?"

"Either. Or."

Her fingers played with the remaining beads. "It's just a hobby of mine. Lots of girls do it. I'm surprised I know something you don't. I'm glad there is something you aren't the expert on," she teased.

Chas looked on with fascination as LaRoux fashioned a leather necklace, a kind of a lariat. It wasn't as cool as Ramie's beaded braids and feather, but his would last longer. She placed it around his neck and kissed his forehead, her warm lips branding his skin. For the rest of his life he would remember the feel of her kiss that June day.

These things bound them together inexplicably. Three was not always a crowd.

A group of Rainbow people set up a temporary camp not far downstream, their own colorful society. All dreadlocked, peace-and-love, with their tie-dye skirts, their Rasta hats. They traveled in late-model, fuel-efficient vehicles and were harmless in their eccentricities, Chas decided. He traded a bottle of Chateauneuf-du-Pape for some weed, which his tribe now smoked, a joint as thick as his thumb as the sun set in the west over the fabled Rocky Mountains.

LaRoux laughed, watching Chas as he drew in a lungful then proceeded to talk. "Chas, you're the only guy I know who can carry on a conversation while holding your breath! How do you do that? How can you talk so much?"

"'Cause he's king of the fucking wind," Ramie sputtered, red-faced, as he tried to hold his breath a little longer but collapsed in a fit of laughter.

Chas's grandmother chose this inopportune time to return his call. He took a big hit and passed it to Ramie.

"Gran! Oh my God, I was so worried about you. Thought you had, like, fallen and broken your hip or something."

LaRoux burst out laughing, and Ramie covered her mouth with his hand. A haphazard wrestling match ensued, during which Ramie dropped the smoldering roach into the matted grass.

"It's her fault." Ramie pointed to LaRoux, on her hands and knees, laughing, gasping for breath. He felt like he should retrieve it, but he didn't want to let go of the girl. He had wrangled her into a half nelson, and she was only pretending to struggle. This—oh, this—was sport. This was love.

Ramie breathed in the smell of her skin, glistening with sweat. He put his lips on her bare arm and tasted salt. A great hot tide of desire rose up in him, drowning everything but his want. His hands slid up under her loose-fitting T-shirt, across the taut drum of her stomach, finding her breasts, two ripe peaches waiting to be picked. Suddenly he couldn't breathe. He found himself doubled over—gasping, groaning— his stomach burning and the fire in his groin forgotten.

"What was that for?" he gasped when he could draw breath.

"You know damn well what that was for! I like you, Ramie Redfeather, I like you a lot. But don't get ideas, you hear?" She brushed her shining hair back; her face was flushed, her eyes snapped. "Just so you know, I know tae kwon do."

"Imagine that," he choked, staring down at those hands, like two small, white starfish, fingertips coming to delicate blue-tipped points. "I'd consider myself very lucky if you'd kick my ass, girl."

"Try that again and I will." She crouched, hands up in front of her face in a defensive martial arts stance. "Got it?"

LaRoux liked Ramie, and she had enjoyed their little wrestling match, but she had a feeling it would ruin everything if she allowed it to continue. She had been raised very strictly to believe her body was a temple, and she had already defiled it with a large tattoo and a tongue piercing. *Don't give it away, girl*, Rafael advised. That's one thing about guardian angels; they are always watching you.

Chas no longer heard what his grandmother was saying; he was looking at Ramie and LaRoux and wishing they would stop messing around, it made him feel sick. He ended the call abruptly, his stomach in knots. *They're going to pull the plug. Time is running out. Time is a burning match, how much longer can I hold on?*

"Hey, Chas, what's wrong?" LaRoux was looking at him all tender and concerned; he couldn't bear it. He realized he was shaking. He was dangerously close to tears, but he managed to pull himself together. There was no way he could tell them about his mother; they had no clue what it was like. His family was so messed up, not at all like other people's families, and now his mother was going to die, though if he hadn't found her when he did, she would probably already be dead. And now he was saving her again by not coming home, he was giving her a chance to wake up and live—one last chance. No, he could not tell them how it was with his mother. He wouldn't be able to bear their slack-jawed shock or their mumbled sympathies, it would ruin everything. Chas was imperturbable, in control, in charge. Chas was the producer, director, screenwriter, and principal actor of this show. Chas must not crumble.

15

"Mind your step, floor's wet." Peggy was mopping the floor inside Ziggies, getting it done to Steven Tyler singing "Dude (Looks Like a Lady)" on the classic rock station. She paused, leaning against the mop handle. "Can I help you kids?"

"We were in here a few nights ago," said Ramie, surprising Chas and LaRoux by taking the initiative, which was generally Chas's role. "We're looking for Redfeather. Hoping you might have heard from him. Wondering if he's around."

The bartender pushed a wisp of hair out of her eyes with the back of her hand. "He never showed up, but he did call. Said he had to fire his agent for double booking him. Said he was playing another gig somewhere—oh, he was full of apology. Or full of something."

"Did he say where?"

"Where, what?"

"Where he was when he called? Where his other gig was? We need a clue."

Peggy shook her head. "I don't think he actually said. Down in his homelands, I assumed. That's where he always used to run to."

"His homelands?" said Chas. "Where's that?"

"He calls it the Apacheria. Somewhere in Arizona or New Mexico. Or Texas, maybe." She shrugged. "I don't keep track of him like I used to. I broke that habit long ago."

Ramie felt that old disappointment coming back home, like a bad smell that settles into the carpet and furniture. A lingering odor you could never quite get rid of.

"I wish I could tell you more, but that's all he said. Left me a message on the bar's answering machine but didn't leave a call-back number. Typical."

They stood there, the three of them, wondering what to do.

"Do you need a singer tonight?" LaRoux asked. "'Cause I'm available."

"Sorry, honey, but we're covered for the next coupla weeks." Peggy plunged the string mop back into the bucket of dirty water and swished it around. "'Course you're welcome to come sing on Wednesday. That's open mike night. I can't pay you nothin', but we pass the hat and the musicians all split the take." She shrugged. "You might make ten bucks—fifteen on a good night. Soft drinks on the house. Wednesday nights is always a hoot."

Fifteen dollars didn't sound like much to LaRoux, who still had two twenty-dollar bills sewn into the pocket of her cargo pants. Besides, she had to get to Austin; the music festival was less than a week away. In one week her life would change forever, of that she was certain. It was time to leave Denver, to leave her new friends if need be.

She had a little crush in her heart for both of them. Chas was short and slight of build, just a little taller than she was. And he was smart—really smart—though he could be a smart-ass too. His complexion was kind of bad, and his teeth were crooked, but he had nice eyes. Eyes you could trust. Fringed with thick, soft lashes. Then there was Ramie: tall with square shoulders and manly, even though he was a year younger than she was. He didn't say much; she liked that, except she wasn't sure what he was thinking. He was good-looking—in an exotic sort of way—with his broad forehead and high cheekbones, his hair like tangled copper wire.

She weighed the pros and cons and decided she liked them both. But three was a perfect number, and she didn't want to spoil the balance of power. Two boys and a girl. To be the only girl, that gave her an advantage, she felt. For once in her life, she held the cards. She called the shots.

"Looks like Denver has dried up," she announced. "Thanks, Miss Peggy, but I need to get to Austin."

"Good luck, girl. If you're ever back in town, stop back and see us."

The boys followed LaRoux out of the bar, into the bright afternoon. "Will you take me to the bus station, Chas?"

"Are you kidding me? No bus for you, babe. Forget the bus, I am personally driving you to Austin. You'll be the only contestant who arrives in a 1960 Cadillac Eldorado, I guarantee you. It's better than a bus, better than a limo, and with me and Ramie as your roadies, your bodyguards—how can you lose?"

LaRoux smiled. "Why, thanks, Chas. I'd be ever so grateful. And if you come too, Ramie, that would be perfect. You are coming, aren't you?"

Ramie hadn't planned to go to Austin. His clothes were dirty and he was nearly broke; he had six dollars left. "Hell, yeah! I wouldn't miss it."

"Let's roll, y'all."

"Only one condition," said Chas, grabbing hold of their shirtsleeves. "We have to swing through Apache country on the way. Drive through the reservations. Maybe we'll find Ramie's father."

LaRoux was game. As long as she got to Austin in time for the contest, she was along for the ride.

Chas stopped at the Conoco station on Thirty-Eighth and Tennyson, holding his breath as he swiped his card to see if it would be approved.

Yes! Ramie and LaRoux washed the bugs off the windshield while the tank filled.

"Nice car," a guy said, admiring the Eldorado as he pumped gas into his shiny new Subaru Outback. "If you don't mind my saying, you ought to put high octane in the tank. You'll ruin your engine using regular unleaded."

"Are you kidding me? I can't afford high octane. I've got a lot of miles to cover."

"Yeah, prices go up every summer. Anyhow, there's a product, a lead additive you can buy to put in the gas tank. It protects your pistons and cylinders. Those old cars were made to run on leaded gasoline. That's a real piece of Americana you got there."

The Subaru driver nodded with admiration, probably wishing he had such a car. But even if he did, would he take it across the country? Chas thought with distain. Nah. He'd keep it safe inside a garage, maybe drive it to the classic car show once a year.

"Don't forget to check your oil," the man said as he got in his economic, fuel efficient, mundane vehicle and drove away.

Chas couldn't wait to get out of the city, onto the highway; he couldn't wait to see Denver in the rearview mirror. He randomized his collection of road trip tunes and Tom Petty's song came up, the one about running on, looking for something, called "Saving Grace." On the seat beside him, his phone played Gran's ringtone, "The Bitch Is Back." He didn't answer it. Glancing in the rearview mirror, Chas felt like somebody was chasing him.

16

Chas drove like a man in a trance, intent on the black, unfolding highway in front of him.

He had a plan. He was going to get off the interstate in case Gran had called the police like she said she was going to. *It's not the car, Chuckie. You need to come home and say good-bye to her. You have to face this.*

The three were in their own spaces, tuned to their own music, their own private worries. The past hung around like the smell of old cigarette smoke; it stuck like chewing gum to the bottom of your shoe. If only you could lose yourself in a song or transform yourself into someone new, some unblemished being, what you truly were inside rather than what circumstances had forced you to become, thought Ramie. Destiny could be such a punk. A schoolyard bully.

Miles flew by, no one talking, no one saying a word except "Could you turn up the air-conditioning?" and "Is there anything to drink?" and "Are you done charging yet? My player is dead."

LaRoux expected the car would be pulled over any minute. She was sure the whole adventure would come to an end in a carnival of flashing blue lights, a state patrolman's fat face frowning at them through the window. Her fake driver's license, should she show it? Or should she say she didn't have any identification, that it had been lost or stolen? Maybe only Chas would be arrested. Maybe they'd let her go, and Ramie too. But then how would she get to Austin? Would the police take her to jail? Would they let her call her brother, or would they notify her parents? And what would happen to Ramie and Chas? Worrying about it was making her crazy because there were way too many questions she couldn't answer.

The mechanical odometer rolled along, collecting the miles, a numerical log, a tally of Chas's new life: 11,966.3...11,966.4...11,966.5.... The value of the car had certainly declined, but the value of his life's experience was adding up. Chas felt the miles stretch like a rubber band. He loved the geography out here—big sky, big land—room to run. The brain had its own geography, its own horizons, and he could practically feel the new neural pathways forming in his cerebral cortex, the canyons of gray matter deepening as he lived and learned, as he evolved into his true self. He, Chas Sweeney, was an oyster, and his personality was the luminous pearl within, a pearl formed as a defense, protection against a sharp grain of sand. He smiled, pleased with the analogy and pleased with the way the numbers on the odometer kept changing. Driving was the essence of freedom; it was movement, essential for survival. Like his forebears, he was a hunter-gatherer, he was a gypsy, he was a sailor on dry land.

"I'm starving. Is anybody else hungry?" LaRoux looked wistfully at the fork-and-knife symbol on the highway exit sign. She was hungering for Kentucky Fried Chicken with mashed potatoes and a biscuit and gravy.

But Chas didn't want to stop, not yet. "This is like *Easy Rider*, only we're not on motorcycles. You guys know *Easy Rider*, don't you?"

LaRoux sighed. "Let me guess. It was a book?"

"No, *Easy Rider* was a movie. Starring Peter Fonda and Dennis Hopper."

Chas felt isolated from his companions. He was not quite two years older than Ramie, and only a year older than LaRoux, but sometimes he felt like he was their uncle Charles rather than their peer. True, *Easy Rider* had been made way before their time, but it was an American classic, one of the first contemporary road trip movies ever made. Road trips were a rich part of American culture, beginning with Lewis and Clark and then the wagon trains on the trail to Oregon. Only in America could average people explore a continent under their own power, stopping and going at will, carving out their own experience, inventing themselves in the process. He searched for the *Easy Rider* soundtrack on his iPod.

"'Born to Be Wild.' Tell me you don't know this song."

"Oh, *that* song," said Ramie, shouting to be heard over the heavy metal thunder. "Everybody knows that one."

"*Born to be wi-i-i-i-ld, born to be wi-i-i-i-ld.*" They all sang out the chorus; it felt good to let it all go.

Chas beat the drum rhythm on the big steering wheel wrapped in white leather. LaRoux and Ramie ripped on their air guitars. *That's what we need, a little group participation*, thought Chas, happy now they had reunited over an old song, music of his grandmother's generation. They were making it new, like the 1980s movie *Footloose* had been remade. They were making it their own song, giving it their own interpretation.

Outside the window the contrails of jets crisscrossed the sky, wide, wavy chalk lines marking the routes of other refugees.

LaRoux had no idea where they were. "Are we still in Colorado?" It seemed like a very big state. She couldn't comprehend its size. The country was so much bigger than she had imagined.

"We're still in Colorado," said Chas. "But we'll be in New Mexico pretty soon. The Jicarilla Apache Reservation isn't far over the state line. Pull out the road atlas, would you? It's on the floor somewhere."

"Are we lost? Maybe you shouldn't have sold the GPS."

"We're not lost. We don't need a GPS. Did Daniel Boone use a GPS? I think not."

"Do you think the Apaches have Kentucky Fried Chicken?"

"What? No. Well, they might." Chas sighed, annoyed. LaRoux was missing the whole point. "I don't know if they'll have fast food, but they'll have something to eat. Don't worry, LaRoux. Everywhere you go, people have to eat. It might not be quite what you're used to or what you were craving, but there will be some sort of food, I can promise you."

"Damn, you are smart," Ramie quipped from the back seat. "Everywhere you go, people have to eat. You are fucking brilliant, white boy. You ought to be a tour guide."

"What do you mean, I ought to be a tour guide? I am tour guide and bus driver, all in one. And this is the great American twenty-first century road trip you are privileged to be part of. But do I get any thanks? Nooo. Nothing but complaints."

From Pagosa Springs they drove south through the Rio Grande National Forest, crossing into New Mexico. Chas felt a little thrill every time he crossed a state line, proof that he was going somewhere; he was no longer just taking up space, he was crossing space, he was moving through time, he was a multidimensional sojourner. "Look, there's the sign!"

DULCE
Capital of the Jicarilla Apache Reservation
Population 2,595

Chas read it aloud for LaRoux's benefit. He knew she could read, but he didn't know if she could read that fast; at the speed he was driving, the road signs passed by in a blink.

LaRoux was feeling a little perverse. She expected something different for a town whose residents were almost all Jicarilla Apache, according to Chas. The town looked much like any other town; they passed a gas station and convenience store, a sports bar, a school crossing sign, and the fire station. Not one teepee. She couldn't imagine Lozen living here, but then she was from a different group of Apaches, and besides, Lozen lived a long time ago in the black-and-white world.

Truthfully, LaRoux was getting weary of thinking about Lozen, Redfeather, and the Apaches. What she really wanted was a hot bath, a couple of Tylenol, and the comfort of her own pillow. She wished she could transport herself back home—invisible, of course, so her parents wouldn't know she was there—and sleep for twelve hours straight—in her own bedroom. In her imagination she walked around her room, touching familiar objects, squeezing her stuffed animals piled up on her bed. She could imagine the hum of the air conditioner and the smell of freshly laundered cotton sheets.

Chas drove slowly through town, turning down random streets, passing the Jicarilla Apache Nation Headquarters, the Jicarilla Public Library, the Jicarilla Behavioral Health Center. Everything was Jicarilla, which reminded him they were in a foreign land, in a sense. This was a sovereign nation; these were original Americans.

"Keep your eyes peeled for aliens," Ramie said.

"Yeah, right." Chas glanced in the rearview mirror to judge his friend's expression. Was he that gullible? Or was Ramie playing the innocent provincial, the noble savage, as counterpoint to Chas, the disillusioned urbanite-on-the-run? Was this a game of wits for LaRoux's sake? Was Ramie trying—and maybe succeeding, in his laconic backwoods manner—to make a fool out of him?

Ramie shrugged and looked out the window. Chas was getting on his nerves. If it ever came to a physical standoff, a show of fists, or a wrestling match, Ramie knew he would win. He could easily kick

Chas's ass. But Chas had him beat when it came to words. Chas had an armory of words, and he knew how to use them. But words were nothing but hot air. Ramie didn't give a shit about words. And Chas wasn't always right, even though he thought he was.

"There's space aliens here?" LaRoux had no problem believing in extraterrestrials. She herself might be from another planet, a foundling left at the fire station—it would explain a lot. Like her genetic difference, the missing genes on the q arm of the twenty-second chromosome. On her planet everyone had the 22q deletion. On her planet, music was the common language. Oh, and what about angels? They were certainly otherworldly. Maybe angels were space aliens, kind of like missionaries in a foreign land.

"There is supposed to be a secret underground facility here," Ramie explained. "Inside the Archuleta Mesa. A UFO base or a secret government operation that studies aliens, I'm not really sure." Was that flat-topped mountain straight ahead the Archuleta Mesa, he wondered?

"It's just a myth," Chas interjected. "Another one of those conspiracy theories."

"Huh-uh. I saw it on the History Channel," said Ramie. "*UFO Hunters.*"

"Ha! So that makes it true? Because you saw it on TV? The History Channel is entertainment, not history."

"Are you saying you don't believe intelligent life exists on other planets?" Ramie challenged.

"Dude, I don't think intelligent life exists on *this* planet. I'm not saying there isn't life out there in the universe. The Drake equation, have you heard of that? It's a product of probabilities; it suggests that there are plenty of planets in the habitable zone. My mind is open to the idea of extraterrestrial life, but I somehow doubt there's a colony of beings from Tattooine living in Dulce. Or that their spaceship wrecked and our government is studying the genetic makeup of their dead bodies."

"Chas, what did you just say?" asked LaRoux. "Were you even speaking English?"

"The whole thing about the aliens was probably started by the Apaches living here," said Chas. "They have an old creation myth; it involves supernatural underground beings called the Hacticin. Anyway, the creation legend somehow became connected with the science fiction ideology of spaceships and flying saucers."

"You and your hundred-dollar words. How would you know about Apache legends?" scoffed Ramie. "Oh, wait, I know. Wikipedia?"

"Well, yeah. Wikipedia is awesome. Anything you want to know is on Wikipedia. It's better than an encyclopedia, and it's constantly being updated and revised. The world is at our fingertips; we just have to ask. We have instant access to information—it's almost as fast as telepathy. Fucking awesome! The World Wide Web is the most revolutionary phenomenon of our time. In less than a generation, it's changed society, faster than the printing press did, way back when it was invented. MySpace, Facebook, Twitter—"

"Dude, fuck Twitter. I bet you don't even have a signal out here, do you?" Ramie didn't have a computer of his own, he used the library's. But he wanted one in the worst way. A laptop that he could play games and watch movies on. Everybody had computers these days. Computers and smart phones. Everybody but him.

"You're right, I don't have a signal out here. But don't slam technology, don't be such a Luddite. Luddites were afraid of technology. Type *Luddite* into your search engine, you can learn all about them. And how did you find out Redfeather was playing at Ziggies? On the Internet, am I right?"

"Well, yeah. But it was a dead end. I still haven't found him. The bastard's elusive. Some forces are more powerful than technology, Chas."

"I know that. That's why I'm on a road trip, that's what I'm chasing. Life. I'm not waiting for somebody to send me a text saying, 'Hey, Chas, this is your life.' I'm running the bitch down, am I not?"

"Maybe life is all a matter of luck," said Ramie. "Ever hear of Lady Luck?"

"Sure, but they aren't the same. Lady Luck throws you a bone now and again, or fucks with you, depending on her mood. But Fate is the big cheese; he's the man with the overall plan. Fate's God. If there is a God. Which I highly doubt. Fate, Lady Luck, God—they're probably all inventions of the human imagination."

"I don't need Lady Luck," said LaRoux. "I've got a guardian angel who looks after me. His name is Rafael. He's riding on top of this car right now." LaRoux smiled knowingly. "I think Rafael might be responsible for our coming together. The three of us."

Neither Ramie nor Chas had a response for that. Did she seriously believe there was an angel riding on the roof of the Cadillac? Or was she speaking symbolically, taking poetic license? With LaRoux, it was hard to tell.

"That's awesome, LaRoux," Chas said dryly. How about asking him where Redfeather is? And pass me another can of Red Bull, would you?"

Chas pulled into the Jicarilla Motel and Casino and looked for a place to park the big car in the crowded lot.

"What are we doing here?" LaRoux wondered. Ramie just shrugged.

"Finding out shit. Getting the lay of the land. Looking for Redfeather." Chas was exasperated with them, yet he felt responsible for his new friends, for their well-being, for their happiness even. Everything seemed to be falling apart. They were running out of money, they were road-weary, they were getting on each other's nerves. Chas wanted to rekindle that sparkling of serendipity and adventure they had experienced in Denver, that first night at Ziggies. What they needed was a lead, a clue. That, and a good meal.

"You all coming in with me, or are you just going to sit here sulking?"

The casino was a room of maybe thirty slot machines, an electronic symphony of ringing, pinging, and flashing lights. The machines were operated by zombie-like beings who stared at them as if in a trance. Smoking cigarettes hung from their lips.

"I think we found the aliens," said Chas.

"I wonder if those machines take quarters," Ramie said, drifting toward the casino.

"LaRoux, watch him, will you? Don't let the dumb-ass throw away his money on the slots." Chas went to the lobby to talk to the receptionist, a pretty young Native American with sparkly purple nail polish. Her name badge said ANGEL. And she did not know anyone by the name of Redfeather.

"Sorry, I don't think he's from around here. Doesn't sound Jicarilla. Doesn't sound like any kind of Apache, really."

"He's a musician, he plays the blues."

She shrugged. "Never heard of him. But I got two kids, I don't get out much. Except for work."

Chas felt his own smile collapse. He wanted some hint, a clue; a vague rumor would do. Some bit of knowledge to refuel them for their quest.

"There's a bar next door, they have live music most nights. Here's their lineup this week." Angel handed him a card.

Thursday June 12	Aeriax—Heavy Metal covers and originals
Friday June 13	Decades of Rock— Classic Rock
Saturday June 14	Red Whiskey Blue— Renegade Country

No mention of Redfeather. He handed the card back, disappointed. "I really hoped he'd be here. I guess we'll head on down to the San Carlos Reservation."

"Are you looking for a room tonight?" The girl's eyes were the color of a Hershey bar in the sun.

"No. We want to be at one with nature. We're camping."

"We've got one room left. If you want it. The International UFO Conference is meeting here this week."

"Ha! You're kidding me!"

The clerk blinked slowly. "No. I'm not."

"So—is there any truth to the stories?"

"About Archuleta Mesa? The subterranean facility? Those stories?"

"Yeah. What's your opinion about all of that? Have you ever seen anything strange?"

She was silent for a moment. "Well, let's just say we Jicarilla have our own beliefs about what goes on around here. Kinda hard, um, to explain, well, to—"

"To a white boy?" Chas said, wishing he wasn't.

She smiled and lowered her eyes. "Actually, we're not supposed to talk about it at all."

"About what? Does it have to do with the Hacticin?"

"The—what?"

"Maybe I'm not pronouncing it right. I read about them online, the Hacticin. The underground spirits that live below the *sipapu,* the navel of Mother Earth."

Angel's eyes were laughing, and he felt embarrassed. He felt so very short.

The phone rang and she held a finger up, signaling for him to wait while she took the call. He stepped back from the desk, looking around the lobby decorated with sand paintings and feathered dream catchers. He wondered if they were real Apache artwork or imitations made in China.

"Room 138? Hold on, please." She turned back to Chas, wrinkling her brow.

"OK, Mister Know-It-All, so what are you? An anthropology student?"

He was conscious of his crooked teeth. "No, I just read a lot. And I'm on a road trip with my friends. Do you know of any place we can camp around here? We can't afford a motel."

"There's an RV park not far north, maybe fifteen miles."

"Can't afford an RV park. We're tent camping"

"Where are you from?"

"All over. Cheyenne, Baton Rouge, Baltimore."

"But where are *you* from?" Head tilted like a puppy.

Is she flirting with me? he wondered

"Baltimore. I had to get away. Had to get the hell out."

"Where you headed?"

"We're taking LaRoux, she's a singer, to Austin—and we're looking for Redfeather. Ramie's father. Ramie's from Cheyenne."

Angel made a little pout face. "Wish I could go on a road trip. Once you get married and have kids, you don't go nowhere."

She is definitely flirting. A hot Apache chick, married with kids, is flirting with me! He wanted to say, "Your husband is a lucky man," but it sounded too ridiculous. In spite of his gift of gab, Chas did not know how to flirt. He wished he could think of something really clever to say.

"If you want to camp, you can pitch a tent just about anywhere you like. The whole forest is a campground. Take one of those maps off the rack, if you want. Just watch out you don't get abducted." Angel gave him a coy look and his heart started thumping like a tom-tom—not the GPS TomTom, but the drum the natives beat with the palms of their hands to send messages. His heart was definitely signaling something.

17

Chas wanted to buy them all dinner at the café, but the menu was too expensive. They ended up going to the Jicarilla grocery store where they bought a loaf of bread, lunch meat and cheese, and a six-pack of Pabst—all for $9.98. Chas rifled through his wallet for his fake identification card, which the cashier hardly glanced at.

"Do you know of a guy named Redfeather? Raymond Redfeather? He's a musician. A traveling musician. Plays the blues."

The cashier shook her head and handed Chas two cents change.

"It's kind of important that we find him. My friend here, he's Apache. It's his father."

"Well, good luck with that. Fathers can be hard to find, unless they want to be. You might ask Shirley."

"Who's Shirley?"

"She's a medicine woman. And she's psychic. She might know Redfeather." The cashier took a freebee tourist map of Dulce from the stack and wrote a phone number on it. "She lives on the south end of town, right about here." She made an X on the map. "Shirley doesn't do business over the phone. She'll want to see you face-to-face; that's how her power works. Then again, she might not want to see you at all because you're a stranger. But give her a call. Tell her Lena sent you."

It was a silky, cool evening as they spread their picnic on the hood of the Cadillac at the far end of the grocery store parking lot. They opened the mustard and mayonnaise packets Ramie had pilfered and smeared them on the white bread, layering slices of lunch meat and cheese. They quenched their thirst with dripping cans of beer, watching the swallows dive and dart in the plum-colored sky overhead. Nine o'clock at night and there was still a remnant of pale sky where the sun had disappeared behind the mesa.

"I feel like I've been here before," said LaRoux. "Y'all ever get that feeling?"

"Déjà vu? Yeah. All the time."

"You, Ramie?"

He shrugged. Right at this instant he was glad to be alive—he wasn't in need of anything, he wasn't hurting, he was eating a sandwich and drinking a beer and watching LaRoux's bare white legs dangling off the hood of the car, worn-thin flip-flops hanging from her toes. A little scar on her knee, like a sickle moon. He longed to touch it, felt a rush of warmth and desire—was this happiness? Already he felt it slipping out of his grasp.

LaRoux looked down at her legs with mild disgust. She had forgotten to pack a razor, and now her lower legs were sprouting dark hair and there was nothing to be done. She should have bought a pack of disposables from the grocery store. She needed to wash her clothes. They smelled awful.

A 1982 Camaro pulled into the parking lot, windows down, stereo playing, Brooks and Dunn singing, "She gets crazy on a full moon."

Chas was stoked. "What luck is this! Getting hooked up with a sha-man, an actual shaman!"

"Medicine woman," LaRoux corrected, sipping on her beer. She didn't really like beer, but it was a nice change from the wine. A glass of sweet ice tea would be just the thing, but no one out here seemed to know how to make it. The bottled tea sold in stores was terrible. She missed the pitcher of ice tea her mother kept in the refrigerator, a pitcher that never seemed to run dry.

"You guys, this is authentic. Except I can't believe her name is Shirley. That's a lame name for an Apache spiritual leader." Chas pulled out his phone and entered the number the cashier had written on the map, then handed it to Ramie. "Here. Talk to her, bro. Set it up. And see if you can score us some peyote while you're at it."

Ramie took the phone with one hand, showing Chas his middle finger with the other. He hated being put on the spot like that, but when the voice on the other end said hello, Ramie hustled to collect his thoughts. Words tumbled out of his mouth randomly; he knew he sounded stupid. There was a long pause during which Ramie's face felt hot, and he wondered if she had already hung up.

"Come on over, Ramie, but come alone," the medicine woman said. "Have your friends wait outside in the car, this ain't no freak show."

"How do I know this isn't some kind of set-up?"

Shirley sighed. "Because you called me, remember? Look, I can't promise anything. The name doesn't ring a bell, but I'll know more when I see you in person."

Ramie ended the call and handed the phone back to Chas. He was nervous. The whole urge to find his father had kind of worn thin. But it was out of his hands now; it had become Chas's quest.

They found Shirley's house by moonlight, on the outskirts of Dulce. Chas made Ramie take a bottle of Chateau d'Yquem Sauternes to give her as a token of their appreciation. A sort of crosscultural exchange. Chas and LaRoux waited in the car. Chas was wishing he hadn't given his last pack of cigarettes away, wishing he hadn't promised to quit. He really could use a smoke right now.

LaRoux was beginning to wonder if she was still in control of her life, except she had never been in control of her life. But now everything was so unpredictable, and here she was now, sitting outside some stranger's house, a shaman, which was some sort of witch. What did Rafael think of this? Was he still on top of the car? Did he still have powers in the shaman's driveway?

Who was Redfeather anyway? She needed to get to Austin. Chas had assumed control of the search, the hunt, like he took charge of everything. She could tell that Ramie was both irritated by that and yet grateful too. Because if it had been up to Ramie, he would have given up. That was the one beautiful thing about Chas, he kept believing. He was not a quitter.

"If he doesn't come out in five minutes, I'm going in after him."

"What, and leave me here all by myself? No you don't, no sir. I'm coming in with you."

"Look, you have to stay here so you can call the cops if there's trouble. If we don't come out."

"Why wouldn't you come out?"

"I don't know, maybe it's a trap. Maybe it's revenge. Maybe she's got a gun and is crazy."

"Stop it, Chas, you're freaking me out!"

"Sorry, I got carried away. He'll come out in a minute. Everything's going to be fine. We're going to find Ramie's father, and we're going to get you to the blues festival, you're going to kill it. " Chas reached across the seat for her hand and was amazed that she allowed him to hold it, amazed that she returned the squeeze. He wondered if he might attempt to put his arm around her shoulders, maybe even kiss her, would she let him? Would she hit him? Or worse, would she laugh at him?

At that moment the front door opened and Ramie came out of the house, the screen door banging behind him.

"He knows something," LaRoux remarked. "Look at him."

"Maybe it's not Ramie, maybe it's an alien made to look like Ramie," Chas joked.

Ramie ducked his big frame and slid into the backseat. "Well, what are you waiting for? Hit the road."

"Did you find out about the secret underground alien biogenetics facility?"

"Duh!"

"Dude! You had the perfect opportunity."

"It didn't come up, OK? We talked about other things."

"Is she old?" LaRoux asked.

"No. She's young. And pretty. Start the car, let's get the hell out of here."

"Does she know where Redfeather is? Did she tell you?"

"Not exactly."

"What do you mean, not exactly?"

"She doesn't know him. She doesn't think he's Jicarilla Apache."

"Well, that's real useful—not." Chas put the car in gear and pulled out onto the dark highway. He was disappointed in Ramie. He had wasted an opportunity. He probably hadn't gotten any peyote either.

"She said there's a lot of music down south."

"Down south? That's pretty vague. South goes a long way. All the way to fucking Antarctica. Did she say where down south?"

"The San Carlos Reservation. Southern Arizona. Tucson area. She Googled him."

"She Googled him?" Chas was incredulous.

"Yeah. On her laptop."

"Hell, I've done that. You've done that. We've all Googled Redfeather. That's not what a shaman does. They're supposed to—I don't know—eat peyote and consult the spirit world."

"Yeah, well, she found something we didn't. Something more recent. There's a band called Redfeather playing down in Tucson. She thinks it might be him."

"When?"

"Tomorrow night."

"Where in Tucson?"

"Someplace called The Bandit."

Chas's mood brightened. "Holy shit, we have a lead on him. Get on my iPhone and look it up."

"Don't need to. She looked it up on her PC and printed out the map for me."

"Pay dirt, baby!"

"How far away is Tucson?" LaRoux asked. She was beginning to think she should have taken the bus to Austin. This was what her father would call a wild goose chase.

"About six hundred miles," said Ramie from the backseat.

"Don't worry, LaRoux, we'll ride like the wind," said Chas, with new purpose. "We'll be there in no time, then on to Austin. I am your rollin' wheels. Just like Morello sings."

"He says 'I am *not* your rolling wheels, I am the highway,'" said Ramie.

"Whatever, bro. We're composing our own song here."

They drove south on 537, leaving behind neon signs and street-lights, losing the last shreds of civilization. They plunged into a rugged, juniper- and scrub-oak-studded landscape, the vast and broken heart of the Jicarilla Apache Reservation. Ahead, a forestry road led off the highway and into the wilderness. Chas slowed down and put on his turn signal.

18

Chas drove along the rutted dirt road for nearly a mile until the headlights from the main road could no longer be seen. Finding a flat spot to pull off, he killed the engine, set the parking brake, got out, and went back to the trunk for the wine and the sleeping bags—and his stash of psilocybin mushrooms he had been saving for a special occasion. To Chas's way of thinking, camping out on an Apache reservation near a purported underground UFO facility definitely qualified as a special occasion—an epic experience, even—though peyote would have been a much more authentic spirit guide.

"OK, you guys—are you ready to powwow?" His voice rang out through the thin mountain air.

Ramie and LaRoux got out of the car, somewhat more reluctantly. It was after ten o'clock, dark now, and above them was a scattering of shimmering stars.

Chas jumped up and down, rubbing his bare arms. "Damn, it's cold! We need a campfire. Yo, Son of Redfeather! Rub some sticks together or something, would ya?"

"Gimme your lighter, bee-atch, I'll start you a fire!" They exchanged a few fake punches and head slaps, excited by the prospect of spending the night in the wilderness.

"We need something to burn," said Ramie.

"There's plenty of trash in the car. I'll go get it." LaRoux gathered up all of the fast-food wrappers, anything that would burn, and added them to the pile of twigs and pinecones that Ramie set ablaze with Chas's lighter. The flame crackled, leaping up in hot, yellow tongues.

"Quick! We need some wood, some branches."

"That looks like a stick over there. Under that bush, I think."

"Careful! It might be a snake!"

"Shhh! What's that noise?

"What noise?"

They fell silent, holding their breath, huddling close to each other. Long seconds passed; the silence roared in their ears.

"Aliens."

LaRoux dug her elbow into Chas's ribs, she was giddy and nervous. "Shut up, Chas!"

"It's just the wind, LaRoux," he said, hoping she'd poke him again. "The wind in the branches. Aliens breaking wind. Cold alien farts."

"Funny. Not!"

Chas was pleased with his little joke, but the burned trash and pinecones were already a smoking heap of ash. The fire was out.

"We should've gathered the wood first."

"It's too dark to see. We need a flashlight."

"I've got a flashlight app on my phone." Chas pulled his phone out of his pocket. But it was out of power, completely dead. He stared at the useless relic, his disappointment tempered by a shiver of wonder. "Shit, it was fully charged back in Dulce."

"Plug it into the cigarette lighter," said LaRoux.

"I don't want to waste gasoline to charge the phone. It'll have to wait until we're back on the road tomorrow. Tonight, we're out of contact, we're on the dark side of the moon."

128

"Hold out your hand. Some for you, LaRoux. Some for you, Ramie, Son of Redfeather. And some for me. "

"What *is* this?" LaRoux stared suspiciously at the dry crumbs Chas had placed into the palm of her hand. She had been hoping for M&Ms.

"Magic mushrooms. My little treat."

"Oh."

"First time?"

LaRoux had never eaten mushrooms. She didn't even like mushrooms as a pizza topping. While she was very curious, she was also cautious.

"They're completely organic," Chas assured her.

"What's in them? I don't want to freak out or anything."

"They contain psilocybin, a mild hallucinogen. It's a plant. It grows naturally, not like the meth people cook up in their bathtubs or the downers the drug companies manufacture and make billions off of. The Native Americans made use of plants with hallucinogenic properties for the spiritual knowledge it gave them."

"Shut up and eat your vegetables, Chas," said Ramie.

All LaRoux could think of was Satan offering Eve knowledge in the form of a shiny red apple. Although she had recently gotten a large, colorful tattoo and had her tongue pierced, she was reluctant to defile her body. Yet she was sorely tempted, for who doesn't want knowledge? Knowledge of good and evil—who wouldn't want that? Why was it so wrong of Eve to taste the fruit from that tree? Besides, what harm could there be in one little bite? One small little vision, nothing too drastic. A purple unicorn trotting across a rainbow—that would be nice. When she was younger, LaRoux had loved unicorns and felt sorry for them because they had somehow missed boarding Noah's ark and were drowned in the flood, which is why they didn't exist anymore. Noah should have been more thorough; she always held that against him. But maybe that whole flood story was exaggerated. And maybe somewhere a small herd of unicorns lived. Somewhere in the mountains of Chile or with the kangaroos in Australia. Or maybe in the south of France. LaRoux could hear Rafael warning her, but she ignored him. But just to be on the safe side, she compromised by eating just half the amount Chas had given her. The rest she let slip through her fingers onto the forest floor.

The three huddled around the smoking ashes, wrapped in their sleeping bags, sipping a 1990 Chateau Montrose, waiting for the psychedelic mushrooms to work their magic. Ramie peeled the label off the wine bottle, placed it on the ashes, and blew on it. A small, hungry flame rose up and devoured it. Overhead the night sky was different than any of them had ever seen—what strange constellations! Their eyes had changed. They had become telescopic; they could now see to the distant shores of the universe.

Ramie showed his friends where he lived, using the night sky as his map.

"See that bright star there? That's Venus. The evening star."

"Dude—Venus is a planet." Chas was a stickler for details.

"Whatever. If that's Venus, then I live way over there, on Pluto." He moved his arm in a loose arc over his head. "Which is somewhere past Mars and Jupiter and shit."

"I don't think you can see Pluto, not without a telescope."

"Pluto?" LaRoux was skeptical. "How can you live on Pluto?"

"Pluto Street. In Galaxy Estates. That's the name of the trailer park where I live. Galaxy Estates, outside of Cheyenne. That's my home."

"Oh, cool!" said LaRoux, wondering if the mushrooms were taking effect yet.

"Yeah." It seemed cool to him, right then. It seemed amazing. "I live at the far side of the solar system. In Galaxy Estates there's a street named for each of the planets."

Chas took a mouthful of wine and passed it to LaRoux. "Actually, Pluto is considered a dwarf planet, it's not even a real planet."

"Whatever, Chas. Who cares? Pluto is where Ramie lives, that's the point. Where do you live, Chas? What's the name of your street?"

LaRoux was missing her own house on Bayou Circle, a cul-de-sac in The Plantation, a newer subdivision in one of the better neighborhoods of Baton Rouge. She was missing the comfortable routines and familiarities of home, the little things she had taken for granted growing up. Like the well-stocked refrigerator, her own bedroom, her own television, her cell phone that Jordan now had in her possession. The homesickness overcame her like a chill autumn wind. She took a mouthful of wine to warm her body, welcoming the prickling sensations on her tongue and gums.

"Meteor!"

Overhead a fireball blazed across the sky, turning from yellow to orange to green before it disappeared behind the trees.

"Oh my God, did you see that?"

"It looked like a—a comet! A fucking asteroid!"

"Pluto!" LaRoux shrieked.

"A flying saucer. A UFO landing at Archuleta Mesa. I read they found a bunch of mutilated animals somewhere in New Mexico a while back."

"It could have been coyotes that did the mutilating," said Chas. "Or dogs. Or bears. Don't jump to conclusions."

"Man, humans are way sicker than animals. We're the only species that destroys our own kind."

"Actually, that's not quite true. The males of many species fight each other in mating rituals. Bighorn sheep, for example."

"Would you fight Ramie over me?" LaRoux wondered aloud. Chas laughed, but there was an edge to his laughter.

"Would hardly be a fight," scoffed Ramie.

"Freezing my balls off," Chas said, changing the subject. "Who would believe it's June?"

"This ain't cold."

"Shut up and pass me the firewater, Cochise."

"I ain't your bitch, and I ain't your Cochise. You want it? Come get it." Ramie hugged the bottle to his chest and whispered to LaRoux. "White boy's itching for a piece of me."

Chas scrambled to his feet, his head reeling. "Come get it, Apache man. Come on! I'm not afraid of you."

"Shut up, dork, and sit down. Nobody wants to fight you." Ramie was sprawled on the ground, resting on his elbows, enjoying his high.

But Chas wanted to fight. Because flight wasn't working. "Is that right, big boy? Don't you want to aevenge your people? Have a piece of my scalp? Now's your chance, bro." Chas did a little Muhammad Ali dance, jabbing at the air. "Come on, come on, float like a butterfly, sting like a bee. Bap-bap! Right-left-uppercut!"

Suddenly Ramie reached out and grabbed Chas's ankle, toppling the dancing Chas on top of him with a thud. "Shut the fuck up," Ramie growled, shoving him off. "Savvy?"

This was it. This was what Chas wanted—a chance to prove himself, to taste blood and sweat and feel like a man. "Is that all you got, sucker?" He leaped on top of Ramie, pinning him to the ground with a grappling hold. "Bring it on, you flame-headed Apache!"

With a grunt the larger boy broke the hold and the two rolled, legs flailing and fists flying, toward the fire pit.

"Stop it!" LaRoux shrieked, angry and frightened at the same time. "Stop it right now—before somebody gets hurt!" Her voice rang out in the dark forest, and she realized she sounded exactly like her mother. But her protests only seemed to egg them on.

"This isn't about you, darlin'," panted Chas, trying for a leg lock on Ramie's powerful limb. He was a good wrestler, had been captain of the junior varsity wrestling team (that was before he got caught smoking weed in the boys room), but he couldn't keep the big boy pinned. Ramie broke out of every hold he attempted.

LaRoux was horrified at the animal sounds coming from their bellies, the mad force of their bodies struggling against each other as they rolled, all arms and legs, right across the rocks and the still-warm ashes of the campfire. They showed no signs of stopping, and she did what she had once seen her mother do to break up a catfight in the backyard— she got a bottle of Evian out of the backseat and poured it over them.

"What the—?" Ramie sputtered.

"What was that for?" Chas spat, disentangling himself from Ramie's arms and legs. The two lay side by side, blowing hard.

"Y'all disgust me. Who's going to get me to Austin in time for the contest if you animals kill each other?"

"We were just playing," said Chas, trying to catch his breath. His head hurt, the wind was knocked out of him, but he felt much better somehow, in a primal sort of way.

"Just messin' around." Ramie got to his feet and gave Chas a hand. "Man, you're a wiry little fucker."

"And you, Kemosabe, are an ox. I want you on my team every time." The two slapped hands.

Chas grinned. He had proven his mettle, but he was convinced that Ramie could pulverize him if it came right down to it.

"What we need is more wood for this lame-ass fire. Come on, Chas, let's you and me go find some!"

The wrestling match had brought them closer together, LaRoux realized. She didn't understand it, but she was glad.

Ramie started off into the darkness; Chas followed suit.

"Wait! What about me?" LaRoux scrambled to her feet. "Don't leave me! I don't want to be abducted. At least, not without y'all."

The three of them set off with a will but wandered in erratic, inebriated circles, stumbling in the darkness, tripping over rocks and roots, their heads fuzzy with alcohol, calling out to one another like crows, shrieking and laughing as they grabbed hold of branches to keep from falling. High above, a misshapen moon spilled silver light and twisted trees cast strange shadows all around them.

LaRoux felt the warm blood seeping between her legs and staining her underpants. Oh, shit! At times like this, she hated being a girl. A woman. But she was not yet ready to think of herself as a woman. The word *girl* at least had potential. The word *woman* felt like a trap. A dead end.

She hadn't remembered to bring any tampons or pads. At home she always used her mother's. The nearest store was miles away—what was she to do? She made her way back to the car and rifled through her pack, looking for the roll of toilet paper she had taken from the gas station. It would have to do.

And where were the boys? Out roaming the forest without a care in the world, except for finding firewood. But, really, they didn't need a fire for survival, she knew that much. They were out in search of adventure and hallucinations, they were doing man-things: throwing rocks, cutting branches with their penknives, possibly beating back wolves or aliens. And meanwhile here she was leaking blood and feeling crampy and out-of-sorts and a little scared. What if a wolf did come along right now; what if he smelled the blood? Or a bear? There was sure to be bears out here. What about panthers? Snakes? There were snakes out here, she knew there were snakes. Rattlesnakes? Stupid boys out looking for wood, out looking for hallucinations, out looking for thrills when all she wanted was a hot shower, a clean pair of underwear lined with a pad, and the comfort of her own bed, her messy nest of a bed with two squishy pillows and her collection of stuffed animals: Henrietta (a hippo dressed in a pink tutu), Esperanza (a purple unicorn with a sparkly horn), and Bob, her favorite teddy bear.

She began to cry, giving in to the warm trickle of tears that spilled down her face and the back of her throat. It felt good to let go a good boo-hoo in a dark forest with no one to hear her but the trees and the rocks and her guardian angel. *Rafael, keep me safe, see me through to Austin where my real life will begin.* She couldn't see him, but she could feel the vibration of his fluttering wings, a hummingbird's wings, quite close to her ears. She curled up on the seat of the car, wrapped in her sleeping bag, but could not sleep for the drum pounding. Was it the Apaches doing a war dance, or was it the persistent knocking of her own heart?

Ramie found a broken branch as thick and long as his leg and rejoiced at his good luck, letting go a victory yell as he dragged it back to the campsite, cracked it in half with his foot, and placed the fuel onto the smoking coals of the fire, blowing on them to revive the flames. He had only been camping twice in his life, but he was pretty sure that was twice more than Chas had been. Chas didn't know the first thing about making and tending a fire, except for some bullshit he had seen on YouTube. Ramie was glad he had found the first branch—not exactly a log, but it should burn for an hour. Meanwhile, maybe the other two would find something to burn; they were still thrashing about, he could hear them. Ramie stretched himself out across the hood of the car, soaking up what remained of the engine's warmth. Looking up into the night sky, he felt as though he were falling up into it. It was as if up and down were reversed and the only thing keeping him from falling into the deep blackness of space was the hood of the car.

What if I'm alone in the universe? What if everyone else doesn't exist, what if they're just…like…dreams?

He was hoping to see a vision. An Indian ancestor, perhaps. An Indian riding a white horse. Geronimo or Cochise, maybe. Naiche or Victorio. Santana or Magnus Colorado. He had learned about these Apaches from Chas, a white boy, white and spotted with angry red pimples. But smart. That smart, pimply white boy from Baltimore had made him feel proud to be part Apache, made him feel proud to have grown up in Cheyenne.

You must dream yourself into being; you must make yourself. Right now, you're just an idea, someone's fleeting thought.

"My father?" Ramie asked aloud. His own voice sounded rich and deep, like some kind of musical instrument. One of those big, stand-up bass viols.

Whooo, an owl called.

Audioslave's music filled his head, and the words to the song "Show Me How to Live" brought tears to his eyes. The night was black, and the stars were bigger than he had ever seen, and there were more of them. It seemed a foreign sky—the night had such depth to it, like he was looking into infinity. He was in danger of falling into the sky.

Stupid human, you are not yet alive, though you want to be. No one can give you life; you must make it from your dreams. The stars glittered, thousands of eyes staring down at him reproachfully.

"Where is he?" Ramie persisted. "Tell me."

You earthlings and your angels, always wrestling them for answers. What makes you think I know?

"Because you are my hunting guide. Why did he leave?"

What you seek, you will surely find. Didn't the young Skywalker find his father?

"Don't bullshit me, alien."

Or what, human? What ridiculous threats! You are nothing but a coyote yipping and barking at the moon. I could annihilate you with one well-directed thought.

"Tell me!" Ramie heard himself cry out. Or was he imagining it?

You must create your own life out of the dust, day after day with a hundred thousand breaths; you must be your own father and your own mother.

And then it was gone—the presence, the voice in his head, the energy. Clouds covered the moon, the stars, and the night was deep. Ramie slid off the hood and stumbled off through the pines to find his friends.

If he heard his father's voice, would he recognize it? he wondered. Had he heard it before he was born, through the layers of skin and fat and muscle in his mother's womb fifteen years ago? Was the voice somehow in his genetic code, his coiled DNA; was it similar to his own voice?

Many times he had thought about how it would be, meeting his father for the first time. Now he knew what he would do. He would confront him, he would call him out, he would give him one satisfying punch in the face, knocking him down to the ground. Ramie swung his fists in rage, hitting the face in the bark of the tree, bloodying his knuckles. *This is what it feels like to be abandoned.*

But what if his father didn't even know of his existence? That would explain a lot; that would almost explain everything. Except for the guitar. His mother said Redfeather had left him the guitar—but why? Was it a message, or a command?

You can find me through this guitar. Our lineage can be traced in music, not blood and bone. If you want to hear my voice, play the chords. If you need my guidance, sing the song.

But Ramie couldn't sing the song; he was mute. He had been born on a distant planet, isolated from his kin, his tongue cut out at birth.

Suddenly there was Brandon, lurking in the shadows, peering from behind the trees, hiding. *Brother, when are you coming home?* The voice was Brandon's but without the defect. Brandon's true voice, a whisper inside Ramie's head.

Come morning, when the mushrooms wore off, he would be left with the wreckage, the litter of unfulfilled dreams, an untidy clutter to be swept under the rug of consciousness.

LaRoux, who had squatted behind a rock to pee, was herself having a visitation, a rather close encounter with a being named Jenn who claimed to be her best friend from a parallel universe.

"But you don't look like an alien. I mean, you look kind of like Sarah Grace Parker, from my church."

Only I'm not. There are so many universes, so a lot of beings are going to look the same. It's inevitable. And the older you get, you'll find it happens more often.

"Find that what happens more often?"

That people you meet remind you of someone you already know. There's a limit to the human genome. Jenn had taken on the voice of Chas, just like in a dream.

"But you're from another universe."

So you want me to look more exotic? Sorry. Actually, I'm a figment of your imagination. It's your fault I look the way I do. You are imagining me.

"I want to see Lozen. Show me Lozen."

I don't know Lozen. If you want to see Lozen, imagine her. You're the creator. You are God's own daughter. You have a guardian angel.

"Yes, but I want to see Lozen, and I don't really know what she looked like. She was an Indian. An Apache. She had special supernatural powers; her hands could feel the direction of the enemy."

LaRoux held up her own hands in front of her face. They looked strange to her, as if they were not her hands. They felt warm and tingled while the rest of her was cold. Her hands were so warm they began to glow, and this frightened her because she did not know how to use this power, she was not ready. Was she channeling Lozen? Did Lozen inhabit her body? LaRoux opened her mouth to sing—but she did not recognize the words that came out. She was speaking in tongues, she was chanting in the Apache language, but she did not understand what it was she was saying. She was mimicking the sounds of a forgotten wisdom; she was merely a parrot. Her arms sprouted blue feathers, but they had been clipped so she could not fly.

Chas's neurons, charged with psilocybin, scrambled the incoming data so that he saw his mother sitting beside him, cross-legged on the ground, yoga-like, her hands resting on her knees, palms up, and where her forefingers and thumbs touched, sparks shot out, like Fourth of July sparklers, the same smell even. Her long hair hung down her back, her eyes were closed in deep meditation. She was on another plane of existence, a state of grace; she was between worlds, but she was still herself. As she breathed, the sound of a flute, a traditional wooden flute playing meditation music, came out of her nose.

"Mom?"

He wanted to touch her but was afraid if he did, she would crumble to dust, she would vanish, or she would wake up from her peaceful state of awareness to the living hell of Want. He backed away slowly, still staring, burning the peaceful image into his memory. At last he blinked and she was gone, the music too. But the smell of burning sparklers remained. Now there beside him was his father, caught in a bear trap, the steel jaws biting into his ankle, a pool of congealed blood. But Charles wasn't howling in pain. He didn't seem to be aware of his predicament at all. In fact, his father was sleeping, snoring softly, and Chas tiptoed away, so as not to disturb him.

"LaRoux, are you OK?

Chas put his hands on her shivering shoulders, his fingers pressing into her flesh.

For once he didn't say anything, not one word, just pulled her close against his chest, his warm, beating chest. She was glad he found her, and she buried her wet face against the warmth of his neck, smelling his shirt, his sweat. And then they were kissing, Chas probing her mouth with his curious tongue, asking questions of her own mute tongue as his hands moved up her back and down her arms, like a blind man reading.

On the one hand, she liked it; she liked it quite a lot. Her inhibitions had been handcuffed and gagged and were watching in horror, and her most private parts had come alive, buzzing and humming, a hive of busy bees making honey.

Chas's hands were roaming freely now, like a pair of Jack Russell terriers crawling under beds to find forgotten socks. It was nice to feel desirable; it warmed her, and the warmth spread throughout her body like a grass fire. Is that what sex was, warming yourself by the fire? Sharing the warmth with a fellow wayfarer? It felt good, but Rafael was frantically whispering that all of this was leading somewhere she wasn't ready to go. She could see her father's frowning face in the cold moon overhead.

Suddenly she remembered the blood-soaked wad of toilet paper in her underpants, and, not wanting Chas to discover that, she pushed him away.

"That's enough. Don't get any ideas."

"What? But I thought you—"

LaRoux flipped the hood of her jacket up and tied it under her chin. "Just go away! Ack! Don't touch me." She stood up and walked further into the woods, her hair all mussed and covered with bits of leaves and pine needles.

Chas stumbled off after her, but she had vanished, so he went in the opposite direction. He was looking for something—what was he looking for? He felt small and ugly, a woodland gnome, one of Snow White's dwarves.

Quit walking, dumbass. People get lost that way.

But I'm already lost.

Go back to the car.

He wasn't sure which direction that was. Clouds moved across the face of the moon and blanketed the stars.

"Hey!" he called out to his friends, his voice rattling his bones. "Ramie!"

ie, ie, ie… His voice returned to him in a series of echoes.

"La-Roux!"

OO, oo, answered the trees, the rocks, the black sky. Chas stood perfectly still, listening as hard as he could, and heard a ringing, like a string orchestra vibrating between his ears. Was this true silence, this pulsating presence?

"Charles Sweeney!"

But this time there was no echo—now how could that be? Had he shrunk so small he was invisible? His voice not even as loud as a cricket's chirp, he was powerless. His friends couldn't hear him; he would be eaten by a raccoon, he would drown in a dewdrop. The vestiges of a dream returned in vivid flashes of familiarity. In his dream he had shrunk completely out of this realm; in his dream he was microscopic, invisible to his friends. They would think he had vanished, they would not be able to find him, and he was calling for help, but no one could hear him. He was so small they might trample him underfoot without ever knowing it.

"Charles Sweeney! Chas!"

An enormous raven appeared out of the darkness. He saw it sitting on a nearby tree branch, a blacker shade of black, a form of knowledge beyond his own. The creature flapped its wings and gazed at him with glittering, terrible eyes then opened its beak and made a sound like an old woman's death rattle. *It's going to devour me, I am doomed to be eaten by a scavenger and become bird shit on the forest floor.*

Ramie was only aware of his heartbeat, the swish of blood whispering in his head, whispering a language he didn't know. Whispering a chant that told him how to live, an audible charm, directions, some kind of prayer maybe? It was both comforting and disconcerting. It made feel like he wasn't alone. For the first time in his life he wasn't alone, apart from the world, behind glass, looking out. Like he was carrying with him the memory of all those who went before, a collection, a repository, a chorus of memory, including the one small voice that was his own that joined in with the others, and he recognized it as his own.

Ramie was kissing LaRoux. Or was he was dreaming he was kissing her? Or maybe she was kissing him. He was flat on his back and she was on top of him, her hair brushing against his ears. Her breath was hot and her tongue was a snake's tongue, quick as lightning. And then he realized Chas was there too, Chas was watching them. Or was he watching Chas and LaRoux make out and he only wished it was himself?

Chas and LaRoux, they seemed so small and weak all of a sudden. Like newborn mice, and he, Ramie Redfeather, towered over them. He felt newly infused with purpose, with the mysterious Force; he was

Luke Skywalker wielding a ten-foot-long light saber. Their voices, their laughter, the titter and squeak of chipmunks, and he could understand their words but not the content. He could make out the words but not what they meant all strung together and spewed out so fast and so squeaky. When he himself spoke it sounded slow and deep, like Darth Vader's mechanical gasp, and it frightened him to hear it coming from his chest.

The night deepened, the earth sighed as the clouds continued to build. Flashes of light, earthshaking thunder, stinging pellets of rain hammered the car, but the three were oblivious. They slept like drunks while Rafael hovered over the roof of the car, watching over them with the patience of an angel. But that was his job; he had nowhere else to be, and time meant nothing to him.

❧

They woke up, stiff-limbed and shivering, Ramie in the backseat, Chas and LaRoux curled in the front, lying like Siamese twins, joined at the head. For a few minutes they were content to lie wordless, listening to their communal breaths, synchronizing them. Needing to pee but not wanting to get up, they waited for the sun to climb over the trees and warm the car like a toaster oven.

When the sun did appear, it burned away the clouds to reveal an Apache sky, a rare, just-washed blue with tattered scraps of clouds. In the light of day, they retreated into their shells, taking with them their secrets. Last night their thoughts and fears had become all tangled up together like they were one organism. They had been like a small colony of ants, communicating through molecules of scent; they had been a hive of bees, conversing through the language of movement, the beating of wings. Then the magic had worn off. The smell of ozone, the flash of

lightning, and the stinging mountain rain had washed them clean and
sent them shivering back to the lonely fortress of their individual bodies, and their desires driven back down into the marrow of their bones.

Raindrops shimmered on the piñon needles, each one a trembling
globe, a fleeting world that would soon evaporate, just as their dream-
like memories of that night would fade over the years to come.

19

After an hour or so, Chas allowed Ramie to take a turn at the wheel. Chas felt like shit; he needed a nap.

Ramie was in his glory driving that classic Cadillac, listening to his own choice of music, a death-metal/thrash mix from his mp3 player. He didn't have his driver's license yet, but he had his permit; he had taken driver's ed. And he had driven his mother's car on the streets of Cheyenne on numerous occasions. Highway driving seemed easy; there was nothing to it. Put the pedal to the metal and cruise. This car was a rocket ship.

Chas, road-weary, with a pounding headache from last night's debauch, was sprawled in the backseat, semiconscious.

"What if we get pulled over?" LaRoux worried. "Ramie, underage, driving a stolen vehicle and all."

"Relax. I'm not going to get pulled over. There's no cops out here, and besides, I'm not doing anything wrong."

Ramie was careful not to exceed the speed limit. He was a good driver, and he loved the feeling of mastery, the way the car responded to his hands on the wheel, his foot on the gas. Ramie couldn't wait until he was sixteen; he had just two months to go. Having a driver's license would be great; having a car would be even better, but he'd have to get a job, and even then it would take him a year, maybe longer, to save enough to buy a used car. Actually, what he really wanted was a truck, a pickup truck. And then there was insurance; his mother had already told him he'd have to pay for his own insurance. It all seemed so hopeless, so unobtainable. Must be nice to be rich and have your parents hand you a set of car keys, he thought enviously. Or to steal your granny's Cadillac.

"What's that you're writing?" Ramie asked LaRoux, who was doodling on her forearm and hand with a blue gel pen.

"I'm working on a song."

"Will you sing it for me?"

"It's not finished yet. I can hear the tune in my head, but I'm having trouble with the words."

"That's OK. Make it up as you go. I just want to hear your voice." Ramie cut off Slayer's musical rage with a touch of his thumb.

LaRoux was not shy about singing, not at all. Her guitar was in the trunk, but she didn't need it. Her true instrument was her voice; the guitar gave her something to do with her hands. She tapped time with her foot, pretended to play the chords she heard in her head, and sang, changing some of the words as she went along. She threw herself into the song, or rather, she let it control her, let it twist her face and jerk her head; she was totally unselfconscious when she sang.

Ramie was practically holding his breath. Her voice was so damn real, so freely given. The words didn't seem to mean anything; he didn't really get the sense of them. It was all about her voice—the sound of it, the texture, pure as an animal's cry—and he wanted her to keep singing; he could not get enough. And best of all, Chas was sound asleep in the back seat; Chas was out of the picture. At this very moment, he, Ramie Redfeather, was driving a car, a classic Cadillac, on a New

Mexico highway, and a beautiful girl was beside him, singing. It was like a dream, only he felt very much awake and alive, and lucky.

When Chas woke up, he noticed the landscape had changed. Now they were driving through a vast, barren basin, speeding through a red, gravelly desert, the surface of Mars. Except the sky overhead was a brilliant blue. They crossed into Arizona on Highway 40 at the Painted Cliffs.

"Oh, this must be Navajo Land. Have you heard of the World War Two Navajo code talkers?" They had not, and Chas felt compelled to educate them. "The Navajo marines were ordered to devise a secret code based on their native language, a code the Japanese couldn't crack. The Navajo helped win the war with that code. And they weren't even citizens, they couldn't even vote."

Ramie and LaRoux were used to these random bursts of information, and they let the words wash over them like the hot air from the open window wings. It was background music

At the rest stop, they ate the rest of the bread, lunch meat, and cheese and filled their water bottles. Chas thought about telling the world he had just crossed into Arizona, but it was a weak urge that soon passed when he got behind the wheel and put the car into gear. He had not texted, tweeted, blogged, or Facebooked for over twenty-four hours, he realized. Did anyone miss his witty status updates, his pics, his likes and LOLs? Probably not.

Arizona looked different; he couldn't put his finger on it. Drier. Harsher. Like an old woman, but beautiful in a stark, dry, skeletal way. They passed the exit to a town called Navajo, they passed the exit to the Petrified Forest National Monument, but Chas didn't stop, even though he kind of wanted to. He didn't even slow down, he had too much momentum. He wanted to drive through the Apache reservations on the way to Tucson, and nothing would deter him.

The afternoon wore on. At Holbrook he turned south and ended up on 180 instead of 77, but that wasn't much out of the way; he could swing back west again in Concho. The road they were on took them right close to the Zuni reservation. There was no time to stop, but he felt a sense of connection just passing by.

Ramie had stretched out in the backseat for an afternoon nap. "I say we go the fastest way we can to Tucson. He's supposed to be in Tucson, that's what Shirley said."

"I still can't believe her name was Shirley." Chas shook his head. Owl Woman or Spotted Lizard would be so much more believable. Maybe she only told Indians her real name. Had she told Ramie? he wondered, feeling left out. Always on the outside somehow.

"Tucson is the only clue we've got, Chas, and we're running out of time. I say, the faster we get to Tucson, the better."

"Yeah, but you ain't driving, are ya, chump?" Chas grinned at Ramie in the rearview mirror.

"If Redfeather is in Tucson, why do you want to drive through the reservations? What's the point?"

"Because it's a road trip, a fucking *road trip*, and it might be the only one I ever get to take, least of all with you people. Following the interstate highways is not a road trip, that's just getting from A to B. And besides, it's on the way. So sit back and enjoy the ride. You'll probably never go down this road again, ever, so look out the window for signs of life."

LaRoux was feeling anxious. The road seemed endless. The odometer ticked off the miles, but where were they? From where she sat, it didn't look like there was too much gasoline left. The sun through the windshield overpowered the air-conditioning; it was giving her a headache. The boys were starting to get on her nerves. Their little quirks, the sounds they made, their dumb remarks and their grunts when she asked a question. She was thirsty and drank the last of her bottled ice tea. How far was Tucson? She was bothered by cramps again and wished they would come to a Walgreens or a Walmart so she could get some Tylenol and tampons.

The country was spectacular, but it was so large, it seemed to go on forever. There were no patterns to the rock formations, the mesas, the jagged ridges—she could make no sense of them. Fear, like a drop of cold water, slowly spread. This Apacheria, where did it end? For that matter, where had it begun? And the Apaches, where were they? The last Apache she had seen was in Dulce at the grocery store.

In the course of forty-five miles, they only saw one other car, an old Bronco, flying along in the opposite direction.

20

"Shouldn't you, like, be visiting colleges or something?" LaRoux wondered aloud. "What if your grandmother has called the cops? What if they're looking for us?"

"The University of Arizona is in Tucson. When we get there, I'll take a photo and send it to her, I'll tell her I interviewed with the dean. UA is a good school. They've got a college of medicine and a college of law there, she'll be impressed."

"Maybe you really should apply." LaRoux thought it might be kind of fun to live in a dormitory with other girls, a shared room all cluttered with textbooks, pizza boxes, underwear hanging to dry in the bathroom. Your friends would be from all over the country, places LaRoux had never been.

She looked around the cluttered car that smelled of body odor and leather seats and realized with a sudden sad wisdom that already the excitement of a road trip was wearing off and college life probably would too. Nothing was ever quite what it was cracked up to be. She would never know what going away to college would be like because she couldn't even finish high school, let alone get accepted into college. LaRoux knew she would have to get by on her voice alone, a gift from God for which she was grateful, but she wondered why it was she couldn't be supersmart as well as have a good voice. Chas was smart. He probably got straight As without even trying.

"What? What are you looking at?" Chas said, keeping his eyes on the road, hypnotized by its straightness, but feeling LaRoux's attention on him.

"What is your problem, Chas? I mean, really? What are you running from?"

For once, he did not have a parry to deflect the question. Her words found their mark, but Chas could not bring himself to talk openly about it. He could not bear the ripple of shock it would cause; he could not bear their helpless pity if his voice cracked and he started to cry. Or worse, their unconcern. What if he spilled his guts and they just shrugged, or told him he was luckier than a lot of people, which he was? What if they gave him that blank stare, that "Who cares, so what?" look? It's a daring thing to bare your soul to someone.

"I'm looking for life on this fucked-up planet. I want to feel what it's like to be alive."

"But isn't there life back where you come from?"

He forced a laugh. "Oh yeah, there's over five million people who call Maryland home. But I'm talking about life, LaRoux. About the verb *to live.*"

LaRoux didn't like it when he talked in riddles. "Are you an only child? You have a grandmother, but what about your parents?"

"Yeah, I got parents. No sibs. My dad's a Rhodes scholar who's been in and out of rehab more often than Charlie Sheen. At the moment he's on house arrest for multiple dewies. Not what I call intelligent life."

"What's a dewie?"

"DUI. Driving under the influence." He glanced her way and saw that she still didn't comprehend. "You know—drunk driving?"

"Oh. I'm sorry."

Her voice was filled with concern, and for some reason that irked Chas. Or maybe it scared him, he wasn't sure. He talked a lot to avoid talking about what really mattered, because if he ever went down that road he might not be able to find his way back.

"Not your fault."

"Not yours either. What about your mother?"

"She's brain-dead. My mother." Chas clenched the steering wheel. There. He had said it aloud.

Brain-dead? LaRoux wasn't sure what he meant by that, but she didn't want to ask another stupid question. It was probably just one of his expressions, making fun of his mother. She waited for him to explain or to say something more about his mother, but he didn't. So she started talking about her own mother.

"My mother is a total witch, I hate her. I mean, I love her, but I can't stand her, you know what I mean? And I don't think I'm really her daughter; I'm pretty sure I was adopted or something. I feel like there's some big secret they're not telling me."

Chas's heart sank like a stone. It was just like he thought. He had spoken the truth, shared his pain, and she hadn't even heard him, not really. Or maybe she thought he was kidding, exaggerating, being sardonic—his usual style. He had bared his soul, and she had changed the subject. *No!* he wanted to scream. *My mother is really brain-dead! That's what the doctors say. She's been in a coma for three weeks, completely unresponsive to any stimuli and without purposeful movement, and they are gonna pull the plug on her as soon as I get back—they're just waiting for me to come home.*

"You want to know why I'm running?" he blurted out, interrupting LaRoux's monologue about her freaky parents and her sheltered life. The words flew out of his mouth, like moths to the light. "I'm running to buy her time, I'm running to escape time, I'm running to find—"

"How 'bout Mexico?" Ramie shouted from the back seat, interrupting Chas's confession. He had not been following the conversation between Chas and LaRoux. He had his earbuds in, listening to his music and looking out the window.

"Dude! Who the fuck said anything about Mexico?"

"I'm just wondering, can we go? I've always wanted to go to Mexico."

"We can't go out of the country, we don't have passports. Do you guys have passports? 'Cause I don't. If I had one, I'd keep driving 'til I got to Tierra del Fuego."

"Jeez, you don't have to get so pissed off about it. Anyway, can't we just drive across the border a little ways?"

"No, 9/11 ruined everything. Now you need a passport to go anywhere. Not to mention the drug wars down there, people getting murdered, their bodies left in the desert. No, it's all fucked for going to Mexico; Mexico is not for us. Which is too bad, because the Apaches ran to Mexico and hid out there." Chas was glad for a diversion. Anything to change the subject. They clearly didn't understand. Nobody could.

"Not listening, Chas. I'm putting my earbuds in, so wake me when we get to Tucson. Unless you want me to drive again." Ramie settled himself, adjusting the sleeping bag that served as a pillow, taking a long pull from his water bottle, and turning up the volume so that the pounding rhythm of Pantera filled his head.

LaRoux was glad Mexico was out of the question. She had had enough road trip adventure; she just wanted to get to Austin in time for the contest. Chas obviously had mother issues, but he didn't seem to want to talk about it, and she didn't know what to say to him, she didn't know the right words.

Chas drove on, thinking how all the good stuff seemed to have happened a long time ago, before he was born. History—the past, his own past—seemed an unfortunate accident. The present felt same-old, same-old, same-old. He wanted to break out of today; today was like hot road tar stuck to the tires, slowing him down. Tomorrow, that was his destination. The future was vast—big and open—beautiful. A little dangerous, like the desert itself, but where anything was possible.

If only he could pull back on the wheel and the car would lift off, take flight. It would be like in his dreams, his flying dreams, and he'd be able to go anywhere, he wouldn't be limited by the straight, flat highway that was the never-ending present. If only his mother hadn't done what she did, ruined her life and his with the pills and the booze—he hated her for that. And he was ashamed of his hate because he wanted to love her; he wanted to be filled with nothing but love and respect for his mother who lay sleeping in a coma and would soon die when they turned off the machine—the ventilator—that was filling her lungs with puffs of air. Now he had to live for both of them, which meant he had to live double deep and to the max.

21

Chas came to consciousness, out of his daydream, his road trance, wondering how long he had been in that state of mind. Had he actually fallen asleep at the wheel? How much time had passed, he had no idea. Five minutes or fifty? The landscape was more or less the same, there were still no other cars in sight. Ahead, far in the distance, he saw a ridge of ragged gray rock, a sawtooth silhouette that looked like a stegosaurus's backbone. He saw no sign of man but for the road itself. No power lines, no billboards, no contrails that he could see through the windshield. A soaring raptor and a few puffy white clouds like a scattered herd of sheep.

His companions slept, and Chas was alone with his thoughts. He was tired of his music collection, all 789 songs on his iPhone; he wanted to listen to something new, something that expressed what he saw, what he felt, what he feared right now. He didn't even bother to search for a radio station way out here, and even if he found one, radio was all corporate now, all prearranged playlists based on some algorithm. Disc jockeys were dead; they were low-paid zombies, pushing buttons and reading from scripts these days.

"LaRoux, wake up. I need you to sing me a song."

But LaRoux slept on, and Chas felt protective of her, protective of Ramie, his two sleeping passengers, his charges, both oblivious to life yet alive in a state of suspended animation. He thought about texting someone, about posting a Twitter update or taking a photo out the windshield for his blog, but the virtual world was losing its grip on him. Instead, he drove on, faster, but it didn't seem like he was going as fast as the speedometer indicated.

Time stood still; he could not escape the present moment. He thought of his mother who lay in her death-like trance. Maybe death was just the absence of time. Maybe time was the hell the living had to endure, and sleep was just a little respite, a little reprieve. Right now the others were sleeping, and Chas was living this stretch of highway for all of them. Nothing made any sense.

On and on, miles and miles. He imagined he was stationary and the landscape was computer-generated and made to look like he was moving. Maybe this was all a set-up, like—what was the name of that movie? Starring Jim Carrey? Where the guy lived his whole life on a movie set but didn't know it? *The Truman Show.* Or—maybe aliens had been in control of his life all along. They'd summoned him to Dulce, they did something to him last night, implanted something in his brain, and now he was being sent to Tucson for some purpose of theirs. It would make a great movie; he began to plot it in his mind and cast the characters.

Suddenly the dinosaur's backbone was much closer, much larger, the road would cross it. He hadn't passed another vehicle since—when? Nothing to do but go on. Still, he wished he hadn't sold the GPS. The road atlas was on the floor on the passenger side. He should stop and check it, but he didn't want to stop, couldn't bring himself to slow down. Just keep going; this road has to come out somewhere. There are no roads to nowhere. Quarter of a tank of gas—shit! Don't think about it, just keep moving, keep covering ground. Somehow he was not where he expected to be. For once Chas wasn't sure where he was, and this was both unsettling and thrilling at once.

"Where are we?" LaRoux sat up. The afternoon desert sun had burned her arm and face, right through the window. In the backseat Ramie slept on, oblivious.

"Grab me the map, would you? The atlas? It's on the floor somewhere."

"Are we lost?" She rooted through the rubble at her feet. "I'm dyin' of thirst. Is there anything to drink?"

"I may have taken a wrong turn a while back."

LaRoux found half a bottle of water and drank it straight down before opening the atlas and finding Arizona. But she could make nothing of it, nothing at all. She felt the panic rising, knowing Chas was going to ask her something; he needed her help, but she did not know how to use a map.

"Look for Tucson," he said. "It's down near the bottom somewhere. T-U-C-S-O-N."

She scanned the page, looking for the letter T, afraid she would fail at the assigned task. At last she spotted it. Tucson. Put her finger on it. "Got it."

"Good. Now move your finger up a little bit, maybe an inch."

"Straight up?"

"Straight up. Maybe a little to the right. To the left should be Phoenix, P-H-O-E-N-I-X. But I don't think we're anywhere near Phoenix. What do you see? What does it say? Can you read it to me, LaRoux?"

She studied the map again, saying the words silently before she spoke them aloud. "Fort Apache Indian Reservation. And just below that is San Carlos Apache Reservation. Oh, and to the other side is the Tonto Apache Reservation."

"Well, that's where we are, somewhere in the Apacheria. Good job, Lozen."

She felt a flush of warmth but hoped he wouldn't ask her to do any more map reading. It made her so anxious; all of those lines and symbols were so confusing.

"The problem is this," Chas was saying. "The reservations are big, they cover a lot of land. And I'm not sure what road we're on. From the interstate I took 191 south to 67. At least, I think it was 67."

"Maybe you better pull over and study this map yourself, Chas. I need a potty stop, and I'm not seeing any gas stations."

Chas slowed the car and pulled off the road. "Watch out, don't squat on a scorpion or a rattlesnake." He could hear the whizzing sound of her stream, even with the engine running. He tried to focus on the map. Clearly, the road atlas didn't show every road, the scale was too big. Where were they?

It was late in the afternoon, the sun was nearing the horizon, he knew which way was west. The sun was on his right, so that meant he was heading south. He thought he was on the road to Globe, a copper mining town on the edge of the reservation. But he couldn't be sure.

LaRoux got back into the front seat and buckled her seat belt. "My, it sure is hot out there."

In the backseat Ramie came to life with a groan. "Are we there yet?"

The road, as it snaked its way into the rocky uplift, was quickly deteriorating.

Suddenly the asphalt ended, a hand-painted wooden sign with a warning: UNPAVED ROAD NEXT 22 MILES—BEWARE OF WASHOUTS! The nervousness set in. Chas knew he had taken a wrong road, but it must have been way back, maybe a hundred miles ago. He didn't want to turn around and backtrack; he didn't think he had enough gasoline. Best to press on. Twenty-two miles wasn't that far; surely there was a town on the other side of this mountain range.

The hard-packed road felt like corrugated metal, rattling their bones as Chas sped over it. Sunset was a blaze of pink, orange, and purple, like fish scales.

"I think we should turn around," LaRoux said. "I'm feeling uneasy."

"We're almost out of gas," said Ramie, looking over his shoulder.

Chas gritted his teeth. "I know that! I've been driving for, like, hours; don't you think I know we're low on gas?"

"Well, why didn't you stop and get gas?"

"Because we haven't passed a station in two hundred miles! Because I somehow fucked up and got us lost, so shoot me, OK? Put me out of my misery."

"Watch out for that dog," warned LaRoux.

Chas swerved, narrowly missing a thin, shaggy creature loping across the road.

"That's not a dog, that's a coyote," said Ramie. The animal glanced back at them before it disappeared into the ravine, giving it a human-like quality.

"Did you see that?"

"Keep your eyes on the road," LaRoux pleaded. "There's, like, no guardrails."

It was getting dark. Chas turned his headlights on. The road snaked its way up then down, hugging the contours of the jagged mountains, an uplift with no end in sight. He was certain they were going to run out of gas, and then what would they do? There was no cell phone reception out here; they'd have to wait until somebody came along.

"Slow down, Chas. Oh, look out!" LaRoux saw what was coming and closed her eyes.

"Oh, shit," Ramie whispered.

Chas was going too fast when he hit the washout where an earlier cloudburst had sent a tumult of water down the side of the ridge, leaving ruts and a rubble of rocks in its wake. He braked hard and swerved to avoid a boulder in the middle of the road. It all seemed to happen in slow motion: Chas braking, swerving, losing control. He was going to crash, and he felt really bad about that. He kept trying to steer, but the car was not responding; it felt like a bad dream.

In the backseat Ramie saw what was happening and instinctively braced himself. *God damn you, Chas,* he thought as the car rolled over the edge of the ravine, throwing him around like a sneaker in the clothes dryer, tumbling, tumbling, *we're all gonna die.* His last thought was of Brandon; his brother would miss him. Except he didn't die. He was still alive when at last the car came to a rest, upside-down, against a creosote shrub.

"Get out!" Ramie heard himself shout. "We've got to get out of the car!"

Chas could taste blood in his mouth. His hands shook so hard he could hardly move, but he turned off the ignition, pulled out the keys, managed to unbuckle his seat belt, and caught himself as he fell from the seat to the roof.

"Are you guys OK? Is anybody hurt? I can't see shit!" He fumbled for the interior lights but couldn't find them. Couldn't find his cell phone. "LaRoux! Ramie!"

"I'm OK," Ramie said. "My arm hurts, I think my hand is bleeding. LaRoux! Are you hurt?"

"I don't know, I feel all numb. I feel like I'm gonna throw up."

"We've got to get out of the car!" Ramie shouted, the panic rising in his chest. "We've got to get out before it catches on fire and blows up! Where's my phone? Jesus, where the fuck is my cell phone?"

"Just get out, get out of the car!" LaRoux opened her door and slid out onto the ground.

"My door's jammed!" Chas screamed. "I can't get out!"

"This side, get out my side," LaRoux called, extending her hand to help him, then Ramie, pull free of the car.

"Oh my God," she said. "You have blood on your chin."

"I do?"

"You're bleeding, Chas. You have blood on your chin."

Chas wiped his chin and stared at the smear of blood in his hand. "I'm OK, I'm OK. Are you hurt?"

"I don't know. I don't think so. We've got to get out of here, away from the car before it catches fire and blows up or something."

Slipping and stumbling, they staggered up the ravine to the edge of the road, where they sat, shivering and consoling one another, amazed to be alive. They watched apprehensively, but the car did not catch fire. It did not explode. In the light of the rising moon, the Cadillac looked like the bleached skull of a dinosaur, half buried in the sand.

"I'm sorry," Chas moaned. "You guys, I am so sorry, this is all my fault."

Ramie patted his back. "Chas, it's OK. We're alive. It's all right."

"The road—I don't know what happened—the ground just gave way." Chas looked down at the car, his grandmother's car, a valuable antique and his magic carpet ride, lying belly up in the gulch, wheels in the air like Kafka's roach.

"What are we going to do?" LaRoux wondered aloud.

"I need to go back and find my phone," Chas said. "Hope there's enough of a signal." But he could not summon the strength. His legs had turned to jam; he did not want to move. His eyes were glued to the Cadillac, waiting for it to burst into flames.

Stunned, the three hunkered together in the deep purple shadows of the gulch.

22

"Who are those people?" LaRoux whispered, tugging on Chas's shirtsleeve. No one had heard a car or seen any headlights.

Three figures moved silently toward them, a dog at their heels. Shadowy figures, materialized out of the scrub oaks, the piñon, the still-warm rock. Beings from another planet.

No one spoke. No one moved. No one dared draw a breath.

Chas searched his memory, digging deep into the corners of his rattled, concussed brain, trying to recall a useful piece of advice in a situation such as this. What should he say? He could not think straight.

Ramie was thinking of the knife in his pocket; he could feel it there next to his groin. He could take one of them, possibly two. Maybe even all three. As long as they didn't have guns, he had a chance. But the dog, that could be a problem.

LaRoux was thinking they had come to help, whoever they were. Maybe Rafael had sent them. She thought she saw a glint and a flash of golden wings hovering above them, though it might have been the result of a slight concussion.

"Hey! Hello there!" Chas said, finding his voice. "Look, we've had an accident. I rolled the car."

The figures moved toward them, soundlessly, until they were at arm's length.

"Espanol?" Chas said, scrambling to his feet. *"Hablas Espanol?* Look, we've had an accident. Accident-o, *comprende?"*

"We're not Mexicans, we're Apache," one of them said. "Is anybody hurt?" His long hair shone in the moonlight.

"No, just a few cuts and bruises. But the car——"

"How many passengers?"

"Just the three of us. I'm Chas, this is Ramie, and that's LaRoux. She changes her first name all the time, so we just call her LaRoux."

The dog, a Blue Tick Heeler, started toward them but was checked by a sound, a little yip of a command from one of the men.

"That's Nana. She won't hurt you." He spoke sharply to the dog.

"Can I pet her?" LaRoux asked.

"Best if you didn't," said the tall one. "Give her a minute to check you out. In a way, you're lucky. If you're gonna run off the road, this little embankment is probably the best place to do it. A hundred yards in either direction, you would've been dead meat."

Chas remembered the sheer drop-offs, the lack of guardrails. Was it just luck?

"Where you kids headed, anyway?" the shorter, heavier man asked. His hair was silver, and his black eyes glinted as he stepped closer for a good look at them.

"Tucson."

The three men exchanged glances. "Taking the scenic route, were you?"

"Well, actually I got lost. We're looking for Redfeather, that's Ramie's father. Tell 'em, Ramie. Maybe they know him."

"Raymond Redfeather," Ramie said, daunted by the sound of the name—his own name—spoken aloud. He felt as if he were summoning a ghost. "He's Apache."

The dog, released by a slight hand signal given by the tall one, now sniffed at their shoes and ankles.

"San Carlos?" one of the men said. "White Mountain?"

"I don't know," Ramie admitted. "Actually, I'm from Cheyenne." His knees shook.

"But you think he's in Tucson?"

"He's a musician," Ramie said. "The medicine woman up in Dulce told me he was playing a gig in Tucson tonight." Ramie's voice cracked as he realized they would not make Tucson tonight.

"You can check with headquarters; each tribe has a headquarters. If he's registered, they'll know. Are you registered?"

"Not that I know of."

"I'm Ned Lonetree," said the tallest one. "And this is my uncle, Edgar, and that's my son, Victorio. We were up the reservoir fishing."

"We'll see if we can pull your car out," said the older man. "A tow truck clear out here would cost you your scalps, I guarantee." At this they all laughed, and it felt good. The laughter joined them, made them a team.

The Apaches went back for their truck, parked a short distance back, around the bend in the road. It took some time, but with the motorized winch on the front of the pickup, they were able to right the Cadillac and pull it back up to the road.

The driver's door was stove in and wouldn't open, the window broken into a scattering of diamonds on the rocky slope. Ned and Uncle Edgar looked under the hood.

"See if she'll start."

Chas turned the key, but the car was dead.

The Apaches conferred. "It could be your battery. Open-cell, lead-acid batteries won't work if their fluid's drained out. Or it could be the carburetor is flooded. These old cars, they're sensitive to rollovers, but the body, the chassis, is like a tank. One major dent, looks like, and a few smaller ones. In the daylight you'll probably see a lot of scratches. Looks like you lost your rearview mirror."

Victorio saw it in the bushes, gleaming. He scrambled down the bank to retrieve it, the dog following him.

"We'll take you home for tonight and come back tomorrow morning," Ned said. "Unless you got a better plan. I've got a battery that'll work, if that's the problem. We'll get you back on the road tomorrow. Get your things. Whatever you need for the night."

Chas opened the trunk. It looked like the inside of a clothes dryer—tangled sleeping bags; a jumble of wine bottles, some still intact; broken glass; backpacks. Wine pooled in the lowest corner, a fragrant pond. The guitars were unscathed—what luck! They pulled out their backpacks and took the guitars, climbing into the back of the truck with the dog, sitting on ice chests of dead fish and holding on for dear life as the truck bumped over the washboard road. The moon was a ghostly grandmother watching over them, lighting their way home, turning silver the sword-like yucca leaves and the long, crooked fingers of the ocotillos.

The Lonetrees' house was a random clutter of buildings and sheds surrounded by a scattering of cars and trucks in various states of disrepair, looking like a herd of sleeping buffalo in the moonlight. Inside, the three travelers dropped their packs, sleeping bags, and guitars by the door and Ned's Aunt Lottie examined their wounds by the bright, naked bulb that was the kitchen light. Her crooked brown fingers felt for broken bones, pried into their mouths searching for broken teeth, scrubbed their cuts and scrapes, daubing them with the slimy broken end of an aloe plant.

"You are very lucky, only scratches and bruises," she pronounced. "That is a dangerous road for tourists to drive, especially after dark."

Chas wanted to say they weren't tourists, at least not ordinary tourists on a summer vacation, collecting snapshots and T-shirts and staying at Best Western motels. Yet he was glad to be alive, glad none of them were seriously injured. He was so filled with gratitude for the Indians, he was afraid to speak, afraid he might start crying, that's how fragile he felt.

A young girl peeped curiously around the doorway, her eyes as shiny black as licorice. LaRoux smiled at her, and she disappeared for a few moments, but soon crept into the kitchen to watch.

"Hi, I'm LaRoux. What's your name?"

"Peridot."

"Peridot, I love it. What does it mean?"

The girl shrugged her slim shoulders. "I don't know. It's just my name."

"Peridot, like the gemstone. Special for those born in August," Aunt Lottie explained. "Also known as olivine. Her mother made jewelry."

Made? LaRoux wondered if something had happened to the mother; had she died? She was afraid to ask. But Peridot—LaRoux coveted the name; she wished it were hers. She thought of other gemstones that could be used as names. Birthstones like garnet, sapphire, aquamarine, and amethyst, which was her own birthstone. Amythest LaRoux? Peridot LaRoux? Having just survived a car crash, she felt as if she had been reborn. Far more so than after the adult baptism she had been coerced into earlier this year. She felt deserving of a new name, yet she worried about changing it so frequently. How would her fans keep up if she kept changing her name?

Peridot took LaRoux to her bedroom to show off her beading projects, her rock collection, her pet lizard, her tom-tom, and her Ariel sheet and comforter set. The red-haired, fair-skinned mermaid was Peridot's favorite Disney character. She had never been to Disneyland, but she had the complete set of Disney princess DVDs. LaRoux thought a Pocahontas bedspread would be more fitting, but she didn't say so. She knew what it felt like to have other people, older people, impose their expectations on you.

LaRoux sat on the edge of the bed, allowing the seven-year-old to brush and dress her hair with feathers and beads. She remembered the times she had spent with Maria, the girl next door, playing with Bratz dolls and getting into Maria's mother's makeup, creating their own land of make-believe. Then one day she had not been allowed to play with Maria anymore. And why was that? Was it because Maria was allowed to have Bratz dolls and listen to Britney Spears and the Backstreet Boys? Or was it because Maria's family were Catholic—Cajun Catlick, as his father referred to them, as if that was a bad thing to be. All LaRoux knew about Catholics was that they had a whole bunch of nice saints to plead their case.

Saints were humans, or they used to be, before they became saints. So they understood what it was like to be imperfect. She rather liked the idea of having a saint to tell your troubles to; it was like having a good lawyer with you when you went before the judge for a crime. Your lawyer would understand that you weren't completely innocent, but neither were you guilty as charged. A saint, like a good lawyer, held your hand and spoke to the Man on your behalf. Catholics kept rosary beads, which she imagined were kind of like worry stones, something to do with your hands when you prayed. Catholics also gave angels their due. LaRoux decided that after she was famous she would officially convert to Catholicism. She would write a special song and dedicate it to Rafael, her very own angel.

"Make me look like Lozen," LaRoux said to Peridot. "Can you?"

But Peridot had never heard of Lozen. Now, how could that be? What if she, LaRoux, had never heard of Martha Washington or... She tried to think of another famous American white woman but could not.

LaRoux dug through her pack for the book she had taken from the Denver Public Library.

"Here, this is for you, Peridot. I want you to have it. You have to know about Lozen; she had a brother named Victorio, just like you do. Only Lozen and her brother lived a long time ago. She might be your ancestor."

"Was she a mermaid?"

"No. She was real."

"Was she a princess?"

LaRoux shook her head, feeling dismayed at the question.

"Well, what's she famous for? Lozen."

"She isn't really famous, but in my opinion she should be. She was an Apache warrior and a medicine woman, and she had special powers in her hands to help her know from which direction the enemy was coming."

"Like a superhero?"

LaRoux laughed. "You might say that."

"Who were her enemies? Who did she fight?"

LaRoux swallowed hard. "The white men. They probably had other enemies too, I'd have to ask Chas; he's supersmart. But the white men were the worst because there were so many. They just kept coming and coming."

"Have they made a movie about Lozen? Is there a doll?"

LaRoux sighed. "No. Not yet. But maybe they will. Maybe you could write the screenplay."

Peridot shook her head. "I want to be the star. I want to be Lozen."

While the girls were in the bedroom, Victorio took Ramie and Chas out to show them his pickup truck, a 1996 Toyota Tacoma. It wasn't street ready yet, it needed a new transmission and clutch, but the engine ran fine and the radio worked great. Victorio had it tuned to Apache Radio, a local station that was playing Megadeth's "The System Has Failed." The boys sat in the cab with the doors open, a six-pack of Miller Lite on the floor. Victorio pulled out a leather pouch and a package of cigarette papers.

"Anybody ever tell you you look like Dave Mustaine?" Victorio, behind the wheel of the truck going nowhere, passed the joint to Ramie, who took a hit and passed it to Chas.

"I'd give my left nut to play guitar like Mustaine does," Ramie said in a pinched voice without spilling any of the sweet smoke he held in his lungs.

At this Chas and Victorio broke into a coughing fit, their eyes watering.

"Do you like Slayer?"

Ramie nodded, still holding his breath.

"They're playing Ruidoso this weekend. My cousin Vera works at the casino restaurant; she said she can get me in free. If only I could get there. Until I get the Toyota running, I don't have wheels."

"If the Cadillac still runs, you should come along with us. After we go to Tucson, we're headed east, toward Austin. We could make a little detour through Ruidoso and drop you off. But how would you get back home?"

"I'm not coming back right away. Might get a job in Ruidoso. Hoping to stay with Vera for a while." Victorio had been working for his uncle since he was thirteen, he told them, and he was getting a little bored with taking tourists hunting and fishing. He wanted to see what else was out there; he was itching to strike out on his own. "Maybe my cousin can get us all free tickets to the gig. You want to go see Slayer with me?"

"Slayer? Oh, hell yeah!" Chas and Ramie bumped fists.

They all ate in the living room, the young ones sitting on the floor, a meal of fried fish and cornbread washed down with beer and a bottle of Sancerre that had survived the rollover. Peridot drank Kool-Aid that stained her lips cherry red.

"Now you must sing for your supper," Auntie Lottie insisted, for she had seen the two guitars they brought in with their packs.

LaRoux wondered what she could sing that the Apaches would like.

Ramie played along, strumming the chords as LaRoux sang "Me and Bobby McGee," followed by "That Lonesome Road." Auntie opened a bag of potato chips and brought out more beer, and LaRoux was urged to sing them her new song, the one she had been working on the past couple of days, which was not a traditional blues song (Ramie could not follow the chords or the rhythm), but it was pure LaRoux. Peridot kept time on her drum; it was a whole new kind of music to their ears.

I'm looking for a mirror,
Have you got one
To lend
So I can get a glimpse of
Who I am
God made me from bones and sticks
From precious stones,
Cactus thorns and primrose
Stardust blue and gritty sand
Oh Rafael please stay by me, Lozen lead my hand
Looking for who I am
Who I am
Still looking for who I am

No one said a word for a long minute after she had finished. LaRoux shook her head as if to clear it, like she was waking up from a dream, and the rest of them began to breathe normally again. Thinking, *what was that we just heard?*

The crisp sound of beer cans snapping open, the rattle of the bag of chips being passed around. Sounds of home.

Uncle Edgar, Ned, and Victorio stayed up late playing cards on the back porch by lantern light while the three exhausted travelers slept on the living room floor, in front of the TV that ran on a car battery and, picking up a signal from the satellite on the roof, was tuned to a reality show about fishing. They were instantly asleep, awaking at dawn when the generator kicked in and the smell of coffee infiltrated their dreams.

Uncle Edgar, Ned and Victorio were good mechanics. With a new battery under the hood, the Cadillac started right up. Victorio put five gallons of gasoline in the tank along with some lead additive, and Ned showed them how to keep the battery topped off with water.

"Here, take this gas can and this length of hose. Never can tell when you might need it. Keep an eye on your tire pressure, and every time you get gasoline, check your oil. A good body shop can fix the dent and all the little dings and scratches, but it'll cost you to match up the paint. That's the original paint job, looks like. That's a beauty of a car. If you was my kid, I'd beat your ass," Ned said gruffly, though his eyes danced.

"Victorio, he knows the land. He'll get you to Globe, and from Globe you just follow the signs to Tucson."

The three of them dug in their pockets and came up with twenty dollars between them, offering it to Ned.

"You all are a long way from home, you're gonna need that," he said.

"If you give me your address, I'll send you money as soon as I can," promised Chas, feeling humble and grateful.

Ned shook his head. "Don't make promises you can't keep. I'm not helping you for the money. You understand?"

"I do. Thank you, Mr. Lonetree." He started to offer his hand, then remembered reading somewhere that Native Americans don't shake hands.

Ned saw his confusion and smiled, clapping him on the back. "Drive safe, Chas."

"Kind of wish I was going along," said Uncle Edgar. "Been a while since I took a road trip. Victorio, look after these people. All of you, stay out of trouble." He placed a gnarled hand on Ramie's shoulder. "Good luck finding your people."

My people. If only these were my people, Ramie thought wistfully. LaRoux watched them in the rearview mirror until Chas went around the next bend in the road and they were gone. It seemed like a hallucination, except for Victorio in the backseat. The Apache sat upright, proudly, silently, his earbuds hidden beneath his raven hair. She wondered what he was listening to.

23

The closer they got to Tucson, the bleaker everything looked. Harsher, more haphazard, the rubble of broken dreams strewn along the roadside in untidy heaps: dried bones of abandoned buildings, former gas stations and motels now nothing but dens for coyotes, rattlesnakes, and the occasional homeless squatter gone raving mad from thirst. So many empty shells of cars left like beached turtles, faded metal signs hanging by a screw. This was a land of failed schemes and get-rich dreams that died of thirst, the meanest strip of highway they had seen. Yet beyond the junk, the refuse of mankind, was an abundance of ironwood and creosote, salt brush and saguaro, slowly encroaching, in no hurry to reclaim their rightful place for what was a generation to them. What was a century to the eternal sand, the sadistic sun?

The passing landscape matched the death-metal music blaring from the radio, and the music united them, Chas, Ramie, LaRoux, and Victorio. They were renegades; they were warriors in an apocalyptic world.

Victorio was glad for the music. It reduced the need for words. Words were like bullets fired aimlessly; the collateral damage was seldom seen. Others seemed to be born with armadillo hide that deflected the bullets, whereas his skin still stung from wounds he had received years ago. The driver of the car, the one called Chas, now he was a talker; he was full of words, and only the music seemed to silence him. The girl did not say much, but her words were very powerful because they came from her heart. She spoke poetry without knowing it. And the halfer, the coyote, the red man with the red hair sitting next to him in the broad backseat, Victorio did not know what to make of him but he kept his thoughts to himself; he had built his own defenses against words. Victorio sensed the walls, the battlements constructed over the years. And he respected those barriers.

Victorio had grown up with a grudge toward white people and Mexicans, except for his best friend, Antonio, who was part Mexican and part Anglo, but that wasn't his fault. Victorio was prepared to hate these kids in their wrecked car, but it's hard to hate people you've just rescued, and they were so clueless. Then he discovered they had the music in common, and the girl was so pretty and her voice was amazing, and he'd lit up and passed a joint with them—you cannot hate someone you've smoked the peace pipe with. They meant no harm. They were like aliens from another planet, looking for a new world to survive on, and in the end they helped him out by giving him a ride to Ruidoso. Victorio pulled four cans of ginger ale out of his pack and passed them around. Ginger ale tasted OK even when it was warm.

This Cadillac was his magic carpet ride to Ruidoso; he had been there twice before, he was too young then to stay. Now that he was eighteen, he would get a job, he would stay with his cousin. Vera lived in an apartment complex. She had said she could get him a job at the restaurant as a busboy; she had said he was welcome to surf her couch. Vera had a boyfriend, a Mescalero half-er whom Victorio was curious to meet. He had always had a secret little love for Vera, his favorite cousin.

Victorio was looking for something—something more than a job and a girlfriend. He could not even define it, the restlessness in his spirit, the sharp desire he awoke with every morning, like hunger, like irritation, a pricking, a goading. He felt a need to go beyond the land of his people, to put himself in some sort of danger, to test himself in some way. He felt like a shadow of his father and uncle; he needed to get far enough away to see if he cast his own shadow.

The music connected them; they had that in common. The heavy thunder was their heartbeats, and the guitar riffs expressed their desire to live, their right to live. The raging voice sang the hard truth of their own eventual deaths, as inevitable as the setting of the sun. Music was their language, deeper than a patois. It was a connection; it was the message they all understood. The white boy wearing the black cowboy hat, the white girl with the uncanny voice, and the distant cousin, the redheaded half-breed Apache.

Tucson city limits and the car running just fine, in spite of the scratches, the busted-out window, and the dents in the driver's door. At the gas station Chas's debit card was denied. He knew it was coming; it was just a matter of when. *I'm a shoe-in for the U. of AZ. Please deposit some money in my account so I can get home*, he texted his grandmother. *I'm coming home.*

They siphoned a tank of gasoline from a Christian Academy Day Care van in the parking lot of the Tucson Botanical Gardens on Alvernon.

"The Lord provides," said LaRoux to herself, keeping a lookout while the boys sucked on the end of the hose Ned had given them until the flow of gasoline started, then put it into the Cadillac's thirsty mouth. "Fear not, little flock. Seek not ye what ye shall eat or what ye shall drink."

Chas turned onto Speedway Boulevard—Speedway, now that was a fine name for a street! Six lanes made for cruising, miles and miles of cruising, and the four of them in an Eldorado hardtop, windows down. Goddamn, it was hot! Tattoo parlors, secondhand stores on every block, taverns, pizza, Chinese, sushi, Whataburger, and Eegee's. Look, there's the University of Arizona! Red letter A, Home of the Wildcats. Chas turned off and had Ramie take a picture of him on the iPhone in front of the renowned College of Optical Sciences, and he sent it to Gran, saying, *My interview went well, they were really impressed!*

LaRoux spotted it first. "Oh my god, there it is! There it is! The Bandit!"

"Where?" said Chas, looking frantically on both sides of the wide boulevard.

"There! Pull over, pull over!"

Chas hit the brakes and made a quick right turn into the parking lot. "Good eye, girl. Proud of you." LaRoux had seen it before any of them, had read the letters on the stucco building from far away.

Once again, at the prospect of coming face-to-face with his father, Ramie felt his stomach twist and his mouth go dry. He mentally rehearsed what he would say, but it sounded stupid. Maybe he would let Chas break the ice.

They walked in as a pack; it was too hot to sit in the car or wait outside under the blazing sun. Inside it was cool, and before their eyes adjusted to the darkness, they heard the smack of billiards and Fox news on the bar TV.

But Redfeather had come and gone. It had been a one-night stand, and they'd missed it. The man behind the bar had no idea where he was playing next.

"We got Guns and Posers playing tonight. Five dollar cover, music starts at nine."

"We don't care about who is playing tonight; we're looking for Redfeather. How about his phone number, can you give us that?" Chas was impatient. What the hell was it with this Indian? Always one step ahead.

"Sorry, that's classified information. You old enough to drink? Can I get you something? "

"Redfeather's a musician. How is he going to get gigs if his phone number is a secret?"

"Well, I ain't got his phone number. I'm the bartender, I do the drinks. Manager books the bands."

"Can you call the manager and get it?"

"Who are you guys, junior private eyes? Doesn't he have a website you can contact him on? Everybody's got a website these days."

"Redfeather doesn't."

"Well, maybe he should."

"Redfeather doesn't need a website," said Chas. "He's legendary. He shuns all that marketing bullshit."

The bartender rolled his eyes. "OK, I'll call the manager. But I ain't promising nothing."

They sat in the cool, dark bar, a shelter from the blazing heat outside. Two men in biker attire shot a game of eight ball without ever saying much. The smack of the billiards and the sounds of Southern rock beamed in from the satellite, decoded and amplified by the sleek little box behind the bar. In the old days, it would have been a jukebox, thought Chas, who had seen a real working one at a retro-style diner in Baltimore. The customers chose their music by dropping quarters in the slot, and a mechanical arm pulled an actual wax record from a long lineup of singles, put it on a turntable, and played it. Nowadays, music was chosen for you. Not even by disc jockeys, but by marketing committees or computer programs, maybe. Once again, Chas was possessed by the feeling that he had been born too late, or too early. But here he was, stuck in this time, and what could he do about it? It was like biting into a mushy apple or an orange that had been picked too early and was neither juicy nor sweet.

The road trip was wearing thin, and they were a long way from home. *The bastard stood right on that little corner stage there and sang. And I missed him,* Ramie thought.

When the bartender finally gave them the number scribbled on a napkin, Chas gave Ramie the iPhone. Ramie took it out back into the parking lot and entered the digits, his heart in his throat. But he got a funny sound, and a recorded voice said the number was no longer in service.

"Fuck it," Ramie grumbled. "Let's blow this town."

"Ruidoso," mused LaRoux aloud. "I like the name of that town. Do you think—"

"No, LaRoux," said Chas. "Don't keep changing your name, you're making me insane. You're LaRoux. You're awesome. Be LaRoux."

"Hey, LaRoux, will you turn up the radio?" Victorio called.

"I second that." Ramie gave his backseat companion a conspiratorial high-five.

Soon Tucson was behind them and they were rolling eastward, toward New Mexico, through an expanse of yucca and ocotillo plants.

"Roots of soaptree yucca were used by Native Americans for a ritual shampoo," said Chas. "Mother Earth and Father Sky provided for them everything they needed. They wasted nothing and wanted for nothing and used nothing to excess. Everything in balance, in harmony with nature."

But no one heard him because the music was so loud. Chas felt strangely light, as if he weighed nothing. Like a feather, like a dandelion seed pod drifting on the wind. Distance was no longer an obstacle; he could move at the speed of light.

Over there, that's probably Mexico in the distance, he thought. The land to the south looked both harsh and inviting, a rugged terrain that Chas longed to explore. But he did not have a passport. He would get one, he decided. Then nothing could hold him back.

Chas had heard the stories how his father had taken a road trip through Mexico when he was twenty-one years old; he and a friend had gone south of the border in search of gold—the kind of gold you roll up and smoke. In those days Mexico wasn't dangerous—as long as you didn't get busted by the *Federales* for breaking a Mexican law. Back then, the drug cartel did not exist—or if it did, they didn't shoot up innocent people. And the drugs were more pure back then. Organic. Benign.

His father's traveling days were over; he was confined like a Rottweiler in a fenced-in yard. What did the old man have to look forward to? Nothing but memories and the occasional meat-lover's pizza delivered to his front door. His father's only mind-altering experience these days was cable TV with its hundred and fifty-two channels, of which *Monday Night Football* and *Survivor* were his favorites, although he would watch anything. These days television was his father's methadone, a perfectly legal drug that he used attempting to fill the hole in his life.

To the south the vast Chihuahua Desert, one of the most biologically diverse deserts on the planet. The Mexican wolf once called this place home, but the wolves had all been killed. Creosote, tar brush, and mesquite, and in the distance the rugged Sierra Madres. They flew past a billboard displaying a group of cowboys on horses in romantic silhouette, like a poster for a western movie. NOW HIRING 1-866-525-8848.

"Hey, look!" said Chas, pointing. "They're advertising for the Marlboro Man."

"You gave up smoking," LaRoux chided. "Remember?"

"That's an ad for Border Patrol," said Victorio. "You get hired on with them, you'll be smoking illegals. Lassoing Mexicans."

Ahead, a check point on the highway; the lanes narrowed to one and all cars had to stop. Patrol cars parked in a phalanx alongside the road.

"What's this all about?" LaRoux leaned forward for a better look.

"They're looking for wetbacks," Victorio said.

Chas braked to a stop, and smiled at the three patrolmen dressed in olive green uniforms approaching the car.

"Good afternoon, sir. The only possible aliens we might have aboard are space aliens," he joked. "We passed through Dulce, New Mexico, what, two days ago? And—"

"Out of the car, smart-ass. All of you, out of the car. Up against the wall, hands in the air!"

The next thing Ramie knew he was spread-eagled against the wall of the station. His heart hammered wildly. What was happening?

"You armed, boy? Got any weapons?"

Ramie felt hands patting him down—his chest, his back, his thighs. He thought of all the bad things he had done lately, yet nothing seemed to warrant this. He could see Victorio out of the corner of his eye, hugging the wall.

"What's this about? We have our rights," said Chas, his voice high and pinched as he spoke into the corrugated metal wall.

"What about these two here?" one of the patrolmen pressed Chas. "Where'd you pick them up?"

"These are my friends. They're not illegals, they're Apaches. More American than you'll ever be," he added through clenched teeth.

"Don't get smart or we'll keep you here all day. This sun gets damn hot."

Don't do it, Chas, Ramie thought. *Don't make me back you up. Because I will. We'll go down together.* But it gave him courage that Chas defended him with his words.

Suddenly LaRoux had to go to the bathroom really bad. She started to sing, to calm herself. If they called her parents, it would be all over for her. If they called her parents, she could forget about Austin. But how would they know where to reach her parents if she didn't tell them?

"Shut up!" barked one of the officers. "No singing. You there, hombre." He pressed the end of his club into the small of Victorio's back. "You're the one I want to hear speak. You know English? Tell me your name and address, and let's see your ID, your green card, your passport, whatever you got."

A third patrolman reached into Ramie's back pocket, pulling out his wallet, attached to his belt by a chain. "Nice try with the hair dye and curling iron," he said. "But your skin is a little dark, don't you think?" He rifled through Ramie's wallet, pulling out his driver's ed certificate and his student ID from East High School. A Laramie County Public Library card fluttered to the ground.

The four stood spread-eagled against the wall, the Arizona sun beating down on their backs. One of the patrolmen had Chas open the trunk of the car, and another brought out a beagle to sniff for drugs. Fortunately, they had eaten all the mushrooms and smoked all the pot Chas had brought, and the sour smell of the broken wine bottles drowned out any residual odors. Still, the beagle spent a long time sniffing.

"Charles, this car is registered to a Linda Mallory of Reisterstown, Maryland."

"That's my grandmother. It's her car."

"Right. And she's letting you drive it clear across the country."

"Actually, yes. She is. I'm looking at colleges. We're all looking at colleges. We've just come from Tucson, the University of Arizona, and now we're on our way to Austin to tour the University of Texas. We hear that's a very good school, and if you are a resident of Texas, you don't have to pay tuition, at least that's what I've heard. Do you know if that's the case?"

But the patrolmen were no longer interested in anything Chas had to say. The United States Border Patrol was paid to catch illegal immigrants, not American teenagers joyriding in grandmother's Cadillac. Finding no reason to detain them any longer, they released them. Without an apology or even a "Have a nice day."

❧

Two hours later they were climbing in altitude through New Mexico's White Mountains, almost to Ruidoso, windows rolled down to feel the fresh air sharp with juniper and ponderosa pine.

"All this is Mescalero Apache homeland," Victorio explained. "The Mescaleros made out like bandits." The White Mountains were quite a contrast to the desert land of the San Carlos reservation in Arizona.

They cruised through the town, passing vacation cabins and prosperous motels, cantinas, fast-food drive-ins, and souvenir stores to find Vera's apartment building. But Vera was still at work, and her door was locked, so they partied with some college girls from San Antonio who were staying in the same complex. Jenn, Jayden, and Carmen had driven up after finals to celebrate, along with forty or fifty of their classmates.

Ruidoso seemed to be filled with Texas college students going from party to party. Ramie and Victorio found a little action making out with Jayden and Carmen, nothing serious, just a little kissy-face and hopeful groping.

Chas wished he was making out with one of the Texas coeds, but it wasn't happening. He thought he'd try his luck with LaRoux, but she had curled up on the couch and fallen asleep. He consoled himself with alcohol.

Sometime after midnight Chas, Ramie, and Victorio passed out on the carpet, their bodies polluted from too many cans of Tecate and shots of Jose Cuervo and too much secondhand smoke. Jenn threw blankets over them and thoughtfully left the bathroom light on in case they got up in the night to pee or throw up.

The next morning Chas, Ramie, and LaRoux came knocking at Vera's apartment. She answered the door in her bathrobe and gave Victorio a good scolding as she made them all strong coffee and breakfast burritos covered with New Mexico green chili. One by one they showered and cleaned their teeth, and then they napped, sleeping until late in the afternoon. At Vera's invitation, LaRoux slept in her bed, in a cool, dark room on clean sheets with a purring cat nestled in the small of her back. It was the best sleep she'd had since she left home.

24

The Inn of the Mountain Gods was an impressive piece of architecture, an Apache enterprise that included a casino, event center, hotel, championship golf course, big-game hunting lodge, and a ski lift on the slopes of the sacred White Mountain and overlooking the crystalline Lake Mescalero.

Chas drove the dented, hail-pocked, mud-splattered, dead-bug-smeared Cadillac right up to the grand entrance of the resort. He rubbed his eyes and squeezed his throbbing temples in an attempt to dispel a lingering hangover and his profound disappointment. "This is all wrong."

Victorio laughed. "Wrong all the way to the bank, White Eyes."

"What's wrong about the Indians making a little money?" Ramie wanted to know. He thought it was beautiful, this Inn of the Mountain Gods Resort and Casino. It was a little piece of heaven, and the gambling was what made it all work. He wished he could try his luck; he had a fake ID but no money, not so much as fifty cents to drop in a slot machine. But that didn't matter. They were here to see Slayer, to hear Slayer—amazing that this resort had a two-thousand-seat event center and Victorio had scored free tickets and backstage passes from Vera, who was a real sweetheart about it. The only concerts Ramie had ever attended were put on by a Cheyenne-based underground band, held in a warehouse on West Lincoln Avenue, and routinely busted less than an hour into the show. Backstage passes! Maybe he could get their autographs, or a souvenir guitar pick.

A handsome young Apache in valet attire approached. Chas stuck his head out of the broken-out window, and managed a smile.

"Nice Caddie you got there," the valet said. Eldorado?"

Chas nodded. "Sweet, ain't she?"

"What year?"

"Nineteen sixty."

"Too bad about the door. What happened?"

"Rolled it, back in Arizona."

The valet winced and smacked his forehead. "Ouch!"

Chas pointed with his thumb to the backseat. "Dude in the back rescued us."

"You folks checking in?"

"Actually, we're just here for the Slayer concert, and I'm sorry to say I can't afford to valet park."

"No problem. You can park free in the garage, all levels, just over there. Enjoy the show!"

"They sure are nice here," swooned LaRoux. "This place looks like the Bellagio. Do you think the lake has fountains?" She had never been to Las Vegas, which her parents still referred to as Sin City, but she had seen it on the Travel Channel.

"Nice service station," said Ramie as Chas entered the large parking structure. "We'll be leaving with a full tank, and no one will be the wiser."

They parked and went inside to explore, passing the casino, the buffet, and the gift shop to the grand lobby that looked out over the lake and White Mountain.

"It's beautiful!" LaRoux loved the smooth marble floors, the enormous vaulted ceiling, and an indoor fountain that seemed to tame the out-of-doors and bring it inside where everyone could enjoy it comfortably. And to think the Apache Nation owned and operated this elegant lodge. They had been given the shaft by the whites, and they had turned around and created a gambling haven. She did not see the irony.

They descended the open, spiral staircase that led down to a high-end restaurant where Vera worked behind the scenes, chopping tomatoes, dicing onions, and mincing garlic. She was a prep cook, doing the mundane work for the chefs, who would come in like surgeons, all scrubbed, their instruments laid out for them.

Chas couldn't get over seeing Apaches as valets and bellhops, as concierges, and in security guard attire. It was all a sellout, a base form of capitalism; the Apaches had sold out, they had become like the White Eyes, greedy for gold. They had become their own enemy, it seemed to him. And he said so.

"Well, what would you have us do?" Victorio countered. "Weave baskets for a living? Hunt buffalo? Steal horses and cattle?"

"Yeah," agreed Ramie, siding with his tribesman. "Indians are real people who have to make a living. This is the twenty-first century, Chas." Ramie held mixed emotions about this creation. It was far more elegant than anything he had ever seen, yet it was not what he imagined. He thought all Indians on the reservation lived in hogans, or maybe mobile homes. He had somehow known there was gambling on the reservations, but he imagined Friday night bingo or card games, a few slot machines at the gas station maybe.

"I just can't get over the blatant commercialization," Chas was saying. "Gambling at the base of your sacred mountain. Your own people going broke, selling out to the white man's capitalism."

"But it's our mountain. We get to do with it what we want. We're not obligated to be your version of Apache. Besides—you're getting a free ticket to Slayer, so shut up about it, White Eyes." Victorio punched Chas playfully on his arm, leaving a red spot just below his T-shirt sleeve.

It was all Chas could do not to wince from the blow. Chas held up a two-finger peace sign. "Sorry, Vic." The concert he did want to see, and if the Indians wanted a casino and golf course on their land, well, that was their business. "Thanks, bro."

"Apology accepted. Now how about we go out to the garage and smoke the peace pipe before we go in?" Victorio said, patting his bulging pocket. "Put us in the right frame of mind. Those girls at the party last night were so generous."

━━━

"Where are you going, Ramie? The show's gonna start!"

"I'll meet you guys backstage. I want to go back and get my guitar. If I'm lucky, I'll get Hanneman to sign it," said Ramie, excitedly.

"That would be the tits." Chas tossed him the car keys and gave him a thumbs-up as the crowd pressed toward the doors where four brawny Apaches took tickets, stamped hands, and checked for hidden beverages.

Like a salmon swimming upstream, Ramie made his way through the masses, back to the Cadillac in the parking garage. There he unlocked the trunk, retrieved his guitar, and found LaRoux's gel pen on the floor of the front seat. He'd get all of their autographs and take home a wicked souvenir of this otherwise futile quest. Guitar case slung

192

over his shoulder, he started back up the elevator, but suddenly had to piss in the worst way. He could hear the warm-up act playing. There was plenty of time, he thought, passing the concert hall in search of a restroom. Ahead, he saw the casino and went inside. There had to be a men's room near the gambling floor. All around, the siren sounds of the electronic slot machines called to him. Across the room he saw a sign for Club 49, a bar, he supposed by the stylized martini glass in purple neon. Not the sign he wanted to see; where in hell were the frigging restrooms? Maybe there was one inside the lounge. A freestanding sign outside the door announced the night's entertainment.

CLUB 49
TONIGHT— LIVE MUSIC!
REDFEATHER
ONE NIGHT ONLY!

Ramie's knees went weak and his head spun. *Holy shit, it's him.*

Inside, the buzzing roar of a bar, clink of glasses, rumble of men's voices, sports announcer's voice. The little stage was still dark, but there was a stack of amps and a microphone.

"Can I get you something?" the waitress asked. Her hair was as glossy as a raven's wing.

"I'm looking for the men's room," he said truthfully. "And I need to make a phone call. I'm with Redfeather. I'm the, uh, sound man, and I need to make an important call, but I've lost my cell phone." Ramie was surprised at his own audacity.

"The restrooms are backstage, through that door, and there's a phone behind the bar. No wait—" She reached into the pocket of her tight jeans and pulled out a slim phone. "Here, use mine." When she smiled, her eyes seemed to melt. "My name's Carla."

"Thanks, Carla. I'm Ramie." His body flushed warm.

"You remind me of somebody." She cocked her head sideways to look at him. "Well, except for the hair. The hair makes you look like the Megadeth singer, what's his name?"

He smiled, pleased. "Dave Mustaine."

"Yeah." She smiled again, her eyes squinting flirtatiously. "But he's gotta be, like, fifty years old by now. How old are you, Ramie?"

"Twenty-two," Ramie said smoothly, though his mouth was dry and his fingers tingled. "But I haven't been back to the res since I was a kid. You Mescalaro?" He thought he sounded like Chas, full of bullshit, but he had to stay; he could not get kicked out of this lounge for being underage.

"Lipan, actually. But my ex was Mescalero."

"Well, I gotta go make this phone call. Thanks a million, Carla." He managed a broad smile, thinking that Chas would be proud of him.

In the men's bathroom, he placed a call to his mother. Surprisingly enough, she answered.

"Ramie, are you all right? Where are you? God, I've been worried sick!"

"I think I might have found him." His heart was pounding.

"Found him?"

"My father. I haven't talked to him yet, but I need to ask you something before I do. I need to know why you gave me his name."

"What are you talking about? What are you doing, chasing him all over the country?"

Ramie snorted his disgust. "Why didn't you name me Mark Allen or Brian James or David Mustaine? There should be a law against naming kids after their fathers."

"Look, don't give me any lip, Ramie, you don't know the half of it. I was a kid myself when I had you. I thought giving you his name might keep him around."

"Yeah, well, that didn't work so good, did it?" His words tasted bitter, they stung his throat.

"What you gotta do Ramie, is reinvent that name, go make it your own. What you—Brandon, turn the volume down, goddammit! It's your brother on the phone, and I can't hear myself think. Turn it down!"

Ramie could hear the soundtrack to a movie in the background. The *bipbipbipbipbip* of an automatic weapon followed by explosions, the shriek of sirens. An apocalypse in his very own living room. Ramie could picture Brandon lying on the worn-out carpet amid a debris of junk food wrappers, his heart-shaped face cradled in his hands, lost in the make-believe violence.

"Why did he leave?" Ramie asked his mother. "Was it me? Or was it you? Did you drive him away?"

His words, small explosions themselves, reverberated in the space between them; he could feel the shock waves against his chest. He could hear his mother over the miles, blowing out cigarette smoke in a soft sigh. The sound made him homesick, a sudden longing that swept over him, nearly drowned him. In his mind's eye, he could see her tapping her ashes with her index finger, red and wrinkled. An ugly, worn-out finger.

"If you found him, why don't you ask him yourself? I'd be curious to hear what he has to say."

He heard a long pursed-lip sigh as she exhaled cigarette smoke.

Ramie banged his fist against the stall door, hard enough to numb his fingers. When he came out of the bathroom, he saw Redfeather tuning a guitar, an acoustic with pickups. His back was turned; all Ramie could see was the thin braid of hair hanging down his back. But he knew it was his father; he felt it, some sort of intuition. Or maybe he just wanted it to be his father.

Up close, the man was smaller than he imagined. He was no taller than Ramie himself and already had a stoop to his shoulders. Ramie thought about confronting him right here, backstage, right now, but decided against it. He lost his courage, or maybe he respected the fact that Redfeather had to go onstage any moment. He slipped out, unnoticed, and found a seat in the back of the lounge, where it was darkest. There were maybe a dozen people in the room, and it was sad to see such a small audience. The room was lit by one of those absurd rotating spheres with pieces of mirror that scatter shards pieces of colored light around the room, reminding him of New Year's Eve. He thought of the concert he was missing—his friends singing, shouting, raising their hands making the devil-horns hand sign, the heavy metal salute. He was glad they weren't with him, he was glad they were unaware of his turmoil.

Redfeather came onstage; there was no announcement. Someone (maybe Carla?) switched off the background music and lowered the house lights. Ramie's heart was in his throat.

Redfeather was a solo act, just him and his guitar. He launched into his first number, an old classic, "Kaw-Liga."

It was not the kind of music Ramie had expected to hear, and he was at once shamed and proud, opposite emotions that wrestled in his chest, pounding and thumping. He was shamed by the poor turnout and the utter indifference of the audience, yet proud because the man played his guitar well and he sang with a true voice. When the song ended, he heard someone clapping; it was his own hands, and he was the only one.

"Thanks," said Redfeather with a nod in his direction. "Now I'd like to sing another one of Hank's. About how it feels to be lonesome. Now how many of you know something about that?"

Somehow, Ramie hadn't figured it would be old-time country blues his father sang. But the words hit home, and his father's voice, like LaRoux's, was extraordinarily powerful, in perfect pitch yet wild, like an animal's cry.

Carla brought Ramie a Coke, no charge, and he gave her back her phone with a nod and a thumbs-up. The nice thing about music, he thought, is that it fills the void. No need for chatter; the lyrics, the sound, said it all. He did not trust himself to speak right now.

Redfeather played a few more cover tunes, songs Willie Nelson and Charlie Pride had made famous. The other people in Club 49 showed little interest; they were there to drink and forget. One couple was there to play footsie under the table and make out. It was all rather sorry.

"I'd like to play something a little different, now that I got your attention. This here's a song I wrote when I was a whole lot younger."

Redfeather began to sing, unaccompanied. Just his raw voice. He cradled the guitar in his arms tenderly, like it was a sleeping baby. He sang in a language Ramie didn't understand, and in a strange key. It wasn't blues, it wasn't rock, it wasn't country —it wasn't anything Ramie had ever heard. It was the same whine the Wyoming wind made when it vibrated the aluminum roof of Ramie's home on Pluto Street in Galaxy Estates. The hair on his arms stood up at the sound and his bones hummed. But no one else in the lounge paid any attention to Redfeather singing an Apache song. It was like he was a ghost up there, a ghost only Ramie could see and hear. The same name, the same looks, the same blood—the same fate? Ramie could not tear himself away from the sad spectacle, and when the set was over and his father took a short break, he made his way to the stage.

Up close, Redfeather's face was ravaged with deep creases and smoker's lines, and he had that pained, pinched look in his eyes, the look of someone down on his luck, someone for whom redemption is as unlikely as a winning lottery ticket. There was no question in Ramie's mind that this was his father. His heart nearly exploded in his chest.

"You got a request?" His voice was gravelly and slurred.

"You might say that. I'm Ramie. Ramie Redfeather." Ramie kept his hands in his pockets, but he met the musician's eyes unflinchingly. How long he had waited for this moment!

Seconds passed, a little eternity. Then a flash of recognition as the ghost of a memory crossed his mind. The musician nodded. "You got her hair, I see."

Ramie flipped the dangling locks out of his eyes in one defiant toss. He wanted to hug the man, and he wanted to break his face.

"All grown up, looks like. What are you doing down here in these parts?"

"Looking for you."

An ironic smile flickered across his hard-used face. "Disappointed?"

"Should I be?"

"You've come a hell of a way. How about I buy you a drink?"

"I'm fifteen."

The elder Redfeather shrugged. "You look old enough to me. Hell, you're taller than I am. Come on, let me buy you a beer."

They sat at a table in the lounge, Glen Campbell singing "Rhinestone Cowboy" on the sound system. It all seemed like a dream.

"You like baseball?"

"I don't care much about baseball. I'm not really into sports. Except hockey, I like hockey. It's fast. They hit each other with sticks and shit."

The older man looked perplexed. "You hunt? Fish?"

Ramie just stared. Who but a father would teach him those things?

Redfeather took a long pull of beer. "You like music? You play?"

"A little."

"Good."

"I'm not. Good."

"How much do you play? You want to be good, you got to play. All the time. You got to dedicate your life to it."

"Yeah. Well. I probably don't play enough."

"What kind of guitar you got? Is that your guitar there? Let's hear you play a lick."

"This is the guitar you left me. The Harmony. I don't play too good. Not like you."

Redfeather frowned and scratched his head. "You must be mistaken. I never in my life owned a Harmony. I wouldn't have given you a Harmony."

"My mother said—"

Redfeather laughed softly. "Women. You can't trust 'em. No way did I give you a Harmony guitar. If I woulda left you a guitar, it would've been a good one."

Ramie felt like a leaf, the last dry leaf that fell from the tree before winter. A single footstep could crush him; a puff of wind would blow him away. He felt a tenderness for his guitar, Mickey Mouse piece of shit that it was. Like it was an unwanted child, a stray dog. He realized then his mother had probably bought it with her tips and had told him that story, had made up a myth of his father so as not to disappoint him. Or had he invented the myth himself?

Redfeather drained his beer like a thirsty man and asked Carla for another round, and a shot of Wild Turkey. When it arrived he downed the shot like it would save his life. Wiped his lips, full lips like Ramie's, with the back of his hand.

"What is it you want from me?"

"I want to know why you left." Ramie gripped the brown bottle. He was grateful for the anger; the anger was keeping him focused, keeping him strong. His anger was a force to be reckoned with.

The older Apache met his stare head on. He didn't look anything like that picture of Naiche. He looked like a man who was old before his time. A man who had made so many bad choices he was backed into a corner. A man who had carried a grudge so long it had bent his back.

Still, Ramie recognized his father, and he recognized something of himself. It terrified him.

"Just tell me. The truth."

"Truth?" his father said. "The truth was destroyed for us a long time ago. Look, kid, I really don't remember what went down with that woman. It was a long time ago. She was just—well—you'll find out yourself, one of these days. It had nothing to do with you."

To Ramie's way of thinking it had everything to do with him.

The musician picked at the label of his empty beer bottle. "Look, I didn't plan on having another kid. I was on the road, like I am now. I was married, see? I was married to a girl on the reservation. Hell, we had a kid, a boy, of our own. But I had a band, a good band, and we went on the road. Phoenix, Denver, Chicago. We were going places back in those days."

Ramie's ears rang, his head spun, he felt like he was drowning.

"Look, the only thing I can do right in this world is play music."

"What's his name?" Ramie heard himself gasp.

"Who?"

"Your other son. You said you had a wife and kid on the reservation."

"She named him after me. Damned if I know why."

Ramie dropped his eyes. He didn't want Redfeather to see them brimming. His heart was cracking like brittle candy. But he had to know. "You have two sons named after you? Two sons named Raymond Redfeather?"

The older man's laugh was a dry bark. He shook his head. "You're not named after me. My name's not Redfeather. That's just a stage name. It's not even Apache."

"What's—"

"I don't give that out. My real name. That's private."

"What tribe?" Ramie managed to blurt out.

"Me, I'm Chiricahua, my mother's people were Chiricahua. I never knew my father. Doesn't matter, we're all ghosts now. I can't say what you are, what with that hair and all. A mongrel." He took a long pull from the glass then wiped his mouth with his sleeve. "Maybe I'm not your father. How do I know? Just because you say so?"

"Man, I have been looking for you since I was, like, five years old. Waiting for you to come walking in the front door. Waiting to hear your voice. I've been imagining you for as long as I can remember."

Redfeather rubbed his bloodshot eyes. "Toughen up, kid. I'm not the father you're looking for. Even if I was, you're already grown—hell, you're bigger 'n I am. I can't bounce you on my knee or take you fishing or teach you to hunt. I got nothing' for you." His words were starting to run together, he was pretty well wasted.

Ramie was glad for the darkness, glad for the distance between him and the stage. He felt like Luke Skywalker confronting Darth Vader, only his father was not out to destroy his son—he had simply forgotten Ramie. A light-saber battle to the death would be so much more honorable. The music from the *Star Wars* bar scene came to mind unbidden; all those weird, wasted alien life forms sitting around getting sloshed together in a cantina on some frontier planet.

The script of his life had been poorly written; it was junk. A forgettable, one-star movie. Except he couldn't forget because he was stuck in it; he had been cast wrong. It was all wrong, and he had to change it somehow. He walked out of Club 49, found the men's restroom, shoved open the door. No one at the urinals, no one in the stalls. He went into the last stall, sat on the shitter, and cried. When no more tears would come, he washed his face in the sink. Then, placing his guitar in the trash bin, pressing it gently down into the nest of brown paper towels, Ramie walked out the door empty-handed.

25

Chas, LaRoux, and Ramie were hauling ass in the Cadillac. They had crossed the Texas state line, leaving Ruidoso, Victorio, and Redfeather in the rearview mirror. The song on the radio was Nickelback's "How You Remind Me."

Chas was irate. "I can't believe you found Redfeather and didn't tell us. Why didn't you come drag our asses out of the concert hall? Slayer was awesome, but I would've rather met Redfeather and heard him play."

"No, you wouldn't," said Ramie.

"But that was the whole point. That's what this quest was about. Looking for Redfeather. You've robbed us of the experience."

"Yeah, well, trust me. It was a bust."

"I thought we were friends."

LaRoux had been looking forward to meeting Redfeather too. But she understood the desire to keep one's parents under wraps—Lord knows she wouldn't want any of her new friends to meet her mother and father. If they only knew what went on inside the home she grew up in, they would look at her askance. *Askance*, now there was an interesting word. She began to play with it in her mind. *As cans. Ask Anns.*

"Let it go, Chas. Maybe Ramie needs to keep his father to himself. Like you keep your parents undercover."

"That's different. I wasn't looking for them. I was—we were looking for Redfeather. He's more than Ramie's father, he's an authentic
American, he's—" Chas groped for the right words.

"If I could choose my father, I'd pick Ned," Ramie said. "And me and
Victorio, we'd be brothers. You'd be my adopted brother, Chas."

They sped eastward, across the dusty flats of West Texas, and as the
miles flashed by, some sort of transformation came over LaRoux. Ramie
could see it in her face; he could feel it coming from her. LaRoux was
writing her own story; she was already beginning the next chapter. She
had already moved on, like she had seen her future and was rushing to
meet it.

The car smelled lived in, like an animal's den—it had become
home. Ramie realized it would be painful, their parting, but he couldn't
bear to think of it anymore right then. This was life, this moving along at
high speeds, looking forward to the next stop, grazing at the gas station
convenience store, stretching out in the backseat, the music filling his
head, his bones, connecting him with Chas and LaRoux, connecting him
with the whole world.

Chas was still sore about missing Redfeather, but he wasn't the kind
to hold a grudge.

I am Apache, Ramie thought with a tingle of awe. *Chiricahua*. He
felt a stirring, a curiosity, a pride in being descended from the rare,
old tribe. But he knew he wasn't only Apache. Not purebred. He was
also Irish American, on his mother's side, or maybe it was Scottish or
Scots Irish—he didn't really know because she didn't really know. "I'm
a gypsy," his mother liked to say, though she wasn't a real gypsy, she just
moved a lot.

I'm a mongrel. A hybrid. I'm a new breed entirely. I'm not my father or my mother. I'm not my brother. I'm Ramie Redfeather, the one and only. I'm an original American.

26

This moment she would remember forever. Taking the stage, guitar in hand, the microphone looming in front of her. It was too high, of course; she had to lower it. The lights bright in her face, she could not see their faces, but she felt the presence of the crowd, a thrumming energy surrounding the stage, a throbbing warm hum of a hive, her home. Her brother Luke was out there—she knew it, even though she couldn't see him. She couldn't see Chas or Ramie either, but she could feel them out there as surely as if they were connected by something, little strings maybe, little nerves of silken thread. She knew she was singing good-bye to her friends and that she might never see them again, even though they had exchanged addresses and she had memorized Chas's phone number.

Her hands trembled, tingled, her fingertips were going numb, but when she struck the first chord it went away, and when she opened her heart to sing, the bubbles in her stomach vanished too and it was just like in her dreams. She was singing the dream, the music coming through her, vibrating her bones and filling her skull, and at last there was someplace for the power to go. It was no longer her gift alone, it was something they all shared, and she was the instrument God played, she had been chosen. It felt so right, so good, to sing, and the words, the music, connected them all. She sang a new song, one she had just written in her head, about loving two guys at the same time and not being able to choose between them.

Hovering above the stage, camouflaged by the dazzling halo of stage lights, Rafael looked down with compassion upon his charge. She could be difficult, but he was so up to the challenge.

Watching LaRoux on the outdoor stage that hot Texas night, Chas and Ramie fell in love with her all over again. Just like in Denver when they first heard her sing (just two weeks ago, though it seemed like they had always known her), they were both struck by the naked power of her voice—raw and a little ragged, but perfect in pitch and so uncanny—and the way it burst out of her, twisting and distorting her slight body, as if the song had possessed her, held her in its grip, and now held them all. The rest of the audience seemed to be equally captivated; they were all connected, all feeling the rhythm. Her words were what they were feeling somehow, though the words didn't always make sense. They were proud of her, and amazed that they knew her. She had been their friend and traveling companion, this girl who called herself LaRoux. They had each kissed her, they had both desired her—but LaRoux was not for them. She was a connector. She was the instrument of a truth way bigger than the both of them, way bigger than the whole audience. And they wondered, did she feel it too? The way she connected them all?

LaRoux didn't win the Break Out Blues competition, much to their disappointment. But she did attract a lot of attention—including a reputable record producer who offered her a contract. Her brother Luke took over as her manager, on the spot. He knew just what to ask and wouldn't let her sign anything until they could have an attorney look at it. Luke dealt with the furious parents, who were just a little less angry once they found out their wayward daughter was soon to be a recording artist—and quite possibly a star. Chas was glad that Luke was a capable guy who cared about his little sister, because although LaRoux was talented, she needed some guidance. She had trouble with simple arithmetic, she was unreliable with money, and he didn't want to see her taken advantage of. But now there was no more reason to stay in Austin. LaRoux had her brother and a recording contract. She had her whole life in front of her. She didn't need Ramie and Chas anymore.

It would have been easier for Ramie and Chas to be happy for LaRoux if it wasn't for the drummer from the winning band already macking on her. To their mutual dismay, LaRoux seemed to welcome his attentions—his drummer's muscular forearms draped around her slim shoulders, his huge drummer ego completely overpowering her. Chas and Ramie were already so yesterday, and they knew it. Time barreled on like a high-speed train.

Neither one spoke for several miles. Ramie was so deep in thought he didn't even realize that Chas, for once, was quiet. No music. They couldn't bear it, not yet. Music would surely cut the strings that held their sorrow in check.

"You hungry?"

A slow smile spread across Ramie's face. He nodded. "I'm always hungry."

"Me too. Heartbreak makes me ravenous."

"How are we going to eat? We're broke."

"I've got my bank card."

"Did Gran make a deposit?"

Chas shrugged. "There's one way to find out. We order, we eat, we get the check, and I give them the card. What can they do after the fact? Make us puke?"

"They could arrest us."

"They won't. Not if we don't run. We offer to bus tables, do dishes. We apologize profusely."

"I'm thinking a T-bone steak," Ramie said.

"I'm thinking a rack of ribs. Or shrimp, maybe. Gulf shrimp fresh off the boat."

"I'm kind of glad her brother showed up. I don't think I could've left her if he wasn't there to take care of her."

"She doesn't need him," Chas scoffed. "She doesn't need us. Did you hear her sing? Did you see that look on her face when she walked out on that stage? She's got her guardian angel looking after her."

"She deserved to win," said Ramie. Her guitar playing wasn't so great, but her voice was pure and true.

"Of course she did. But she got noticed, that's what's important. Who cares about a contest? She was offered a recording contract. Mae B. LaRoux is on her way."

"She's probably already changed her name again."

"You got her to Austin, man."

"We did, bro. Safe and on time."

They bumped fists, a conciliatory gesture.

The Gulf of Mexico pulled them both, like any large body of water attracts. The ocean was the place where boundaries ended and where you could leave your pain and troubles in all that water; it would wash you clean. They ate at Doc's Seafood and Steaks on South Padre Island, so close to the water you could smell it. Brooks and Dunn singing "Neon Moon," followed by a whole string of heartbreak songs that hit their mark. Without LaRoux, everything was different. The glow of the adventure was gone. They were left with bruised hearts and empty pockets.

Ramie had never in his life been to the ocean. He imagined it to be like Wyoming, only blue—a vast territory, largely uninhabited though sometimes crossed, ships like wooden wagons laboring slowly under white canvas, hell-bent to get somewhere else. Most of the earth's surface was covered by water, by vast seas, and he was about to see a large body of saltwater for the first time. At night!

On the dark beach, they stripped down to their underwear and ran to the water, plunging in up to their waists. Chas dove under and swam out a few strokes, beckoning to Ramie to follow. They swam out a bit into deeper water, then floated on their backs looking up at the sky.

"It wouldn't be a road trip without making it to the coast," said Chas. "I had California in mind when I started out. Thought I would cruise down Santa Monica Boulevard and swim in the Pacific Ocean. Instead, I turned south in Cheyenne, and here I am swimming in the Gulf of Mexico. Funny how things turn out. Every choice you make changes things completely."

"I thought the water would be colder. This feels like bathwater."

"It's the Gulf of Mexico. That's why they get hurricanes. The Atlantic Ocean, now that's cold water. Even in the summer, it'll shrivel your nuts. I love saltwater! You know what I miss? I miss crab. Maryland blue crab. Damn, we just ate and now I'm hungry again. If we were in Maryland, I'd take you for some good crab. A dozen of those fuckers, steamed with Old Bay seasoning. Nobody can touch the Chesapeake Bay for crab. And Chesapeake oysters, fried or on the half shell—"

"In Wyoming we eat Rocky Mountain oysters," Ramie interrupted with a measure of pride.

"There aren't any oysters in the Rocky Mountains. Oysters live in saltwater."

"Yeah, there are."

Chas made a dismissive snorting sound.

"You never heard of Rocky Mountain oysters? I can't believe I know something you don't!" Ramie gloated. "Dude, Rocky Mountain oysters are cow cojones. Bull's balls."

"How drunk would somebody have to be to eat a testicle?" Chas wondered aloud. "You've never actually eaten one yourself, have you?"

"Sure I have," Ramie crowed. "That's why my balls are so big, White Eyes."

Screaming a war chant, Chas dove on him, sinking him, and the two thrashed in the water, beating on each other. Gasping, choking, laughing, they swam back to shore and dragged themselves from the water, boxer shorts clinging to their thighs, gulf water running in rivulets through the downy hair covering their calves.

"Hey, bro, I'll race you."

They took off down the beach, kicking up sand with their heels, grunting with the exertion, Ramie's hair flying in the wind. Ramie, with his longer legs, pulling ahead, passing his friend, and raising his arms in victory as he crossed an imaginary finish line. Chas gave it the best he had, he put his whole heart into the effort.

27

"She liked you best. Don't deny it."

"Are you kidding me? You're the man with the car. You made it happen. You drove her all the way to fucking Austin."

"But she liked you best."

"I think she probably liked us both about the same."

"Twenty bucks says she falls for that asshole drummer. I'd like to kick his ass. We should have. You and me. Kicked his ass."

"I think in a way, maybe, she did love us," Ramie said. "Just not the way we wanted her to."

"In a way, I'm relieved. It would have ruined everything, you know? It would have changed things between you and me, and I wouldn't have missed us for the world either."

"Dude, don't go all bromance on me. And take that cowboy hat off, it reminds me of *Brokeback Mountain*."

Chas just laughed. "Fuck you, Ramie. I like my hat. You're the Indian, I'm the cowboy. I got my hat and the beaded lariat she made me to prove it. "

Ramie's hand went up to feel for the feather and beads LaRoux had woven in his hair. Still there, though damp and sticky with salt.

They sat on the sand, watching the light dance on the water, having no compulsion to go.

"Heard from your grandmother?" Ramie asked.

Chas nodded, his stomach tightening. "They're going to pull the plug on Friday. Whether I'm there or not."

Ramie didn't know what to say. "What are you talking about?"

"She's in a coma. My mother. She's brain-dead, and they're going to pull the plug. Take her off life support." His voice broke. "She's going to die Friday morning at ten-thirty."

"Why didn't you say something? I've been with you for, what, ten days, and you never said anything."

"I wanted to. I tried to. I don't know."

"Man, that's fucked up."

Chas nodded, his throat thick.

"But what if she doesn't? You know, die. When they pull the plug."

Chas put his thumbs in the corners of his eyes. "Like Karen Ann Quinlan."

"Who's that?"

"Never mind. Doesn't matter. Whatever goes down, I need to be there. Can't let Gran face this without me."

Chas had run, but it hadn't changed anything. He hadn't saved her. Had his mother ever really lived? he wondered. It would be easier to let go if he knew she had had her day, if she had ever been alive, truly alive. Not just walking, talking, breathing, going through the motions. Then he wouldn't have to save her. He wouldn't have to live for both of them.

"What about you, Ramie? You sorry you found your father?"

"Yeah. No." He thought for a minute. "It's like finding out Santa Claus is just some loser in a fake beard and a cheap red suit. Boom, childhood's over. Worse than that. You die a little death, that's what it feels like."

"Maybe we were looking for the wrong Redfeather."

"I sure as hell was," said Ramie. "His real name isn't even Redfeather. That's his stage name." The swim had smoothed the edges of his bitterness, a resentment he long carried in his pocket. He now held it like a stone, like the one in the palm of his hand. Cool and smooth, weighty as a river rock. Ramie imagined himself skipping it clear across the Gulf of Mexico. He drew his arm back and, with a grunt, gave it a good hurl. He watched it skip twice across the surface before disappearing into the water.

"Maybe we were really looking for another man named Redfeather. You, brother."

Ramie smiled wryly. "Well? Did we find that fucker?"

Chas grinned. "I think we might have caught a glimpse of him. A Redfeather sighting. Definitely a sentient life form, I can attest to that." He gripped his friend's broad shoulder. "Come on, bro, let's go back to the car. I'm ready to hit the road."

As they walked back to the lot where the Cadillac waited, Ramie held onto those words. Sometimes Chas was full of shit, but sometimes he said just the right thing. Ramie wanted to say the right thing too, and he thought of what he would want Chas to say to him if their situations were reversed.

"You want me to come with you, man? You know, stand by you when it all goes down Friday? 'Cause I will."

"Thanks, Ramie. That means a lot. Really, I'd like that. But this is something I've got to do. And you have your own shit going on. Court date coming up, right?"

Ramie nodded. "Wednesday."

"Then what?"

"I don't know. Find a summer job. Pay fines and retribution. But I can get my driver's license next month. Maybe borrow my mother's car and take my little brother camping up in Medicine Bow forest. Shoot the BB gun and teach him how to make a campfire. The right way. Like, you've got to gather the wood *before* you start the fire. And no wine or magic mushrooms. Brandon's too young for that shit."

"How you getting back?"

"Same way I started out." Ramie held up his right thumb like a prize. "It's easy to catch a ride. Some skinny little East Coast cowboy picked me up in a Cadillac ten days ago and drove me all over hell and gone."

Chas grinned. "And he's driving your ass home, so put your thumb in your pocket and get in the car."

Ramie ducked his head and slid his big frame into the front seat. "Man, Cheyenne's got to be hundreds of miles from here—in the wrong direction. I'm headed north and you're going east." Ramie had learned something of geography while on the road with Chas.

"Actually, it's one thousand and eight miles. But who's counting? The way I drive, it's on my way. Besides, there's a pair of cowboy boots in Cheyenne with my name on them. They complement the hat. Hand me my hat, would you?"

Ramie reached over the seat for the Stetson knockoff and set it on Chas's head. "Piece of shit. Probably made in China."

Chas grinned and pulled the brim down. Glanced in the rearview mirror and made a small adjustment. "Doesn't matter. You keep going west far enough, you get to China. China's a real place, with real people. Maybe we should go. You and me." He turned the ignition key and the Cadillac came to life, coughing once, like an old man waking up.

"China? You want to go to China?"

"It'll be a whole different kind of a road trip. No Cadillac. We'll be riding the rails instead. We'll be trekking the Great Wall. We'll be riding oxen through rice paddies and shit. We'll be cruising down the Yangtze on a junk. We'll be making friends with smart Chinese girls, they'll laugh at all my jokes, but they'll probably like you best." Chas smiled wryly.

"I want to see it all, bro. I want to live it. You in? The Apache came from Asia, you know? Your ancestors crossed the land bridge during the last Ice Age…"

Here we go again, thought Ramie, settling in and tuning out. Man, he could talk like the wind.

The Cadillac Eldorado sped north along the highway, one headlight burned out and the original whitewall tires humming against the hot asphalt. The windows were down, and the thick night air felt like warm water against their sunburned faces. The dashboard glowed with its cool red lights, and the speedometer's needle was steady on seventy-five. Chas hung his left arm out of the window and felt the force of the air against his open hand, then closed his fingers and moved his hand up and down like a dolphin swimming.

Ramie settled into his seat and kicked off his shoes. For just a moment, he wasn't angry or resentful, envious or sad. He wasn't worried about his court date, or anything else. For just a moment, he wasn't thinking about anything in particular. His mind was in a road trance; he was only aware of the motion, the sensations. The sound of the wind in his ears. Knowing he was going somewhere. Going home.

"Hey, Redfeather," said Chas. "Since you're riding shotgun, pop us a couple of Red Bulls and dial in some traveling music, would you? Got to have the tunes."

"What do you want to hear?"

Chas shrugged. "Surprise me. See if you can pick up a good station way out here in Bumfuck-I-Don't-Know-Where."

Ramie switched on the Cadillac's AM radio and turned the tuning knob, gliding through political scare talk, Mexican mariachi music, Christian rock, and Bible-belt preaching. He was searching the airwaves for just the right song: a song to define this moment, a song to carry them over the next few miles.

They had a long night ahead of them, but it would fly by like the blur of mileposts on the side of the highway. In his mind's eye, Ramie could already see his trailer house on Pluto Street in Galaxy Estates. Brandon was up late, glued to the PlayStation. Mom's car was parked outside. She was already in bed, tired after a long day at work, but she was sleeping lightly with an ear out for him, and she had left the porch light on for his return.

-00-

ABOUT THE AUTHOR

Linda Collison has worked as a registered nurse, a skydiving instructor, a volunteer firefighter, a mother, a freelance writer, and other sundry occupations. Her articles and essays have been published in a wide variety of magazines and her fiction has been awarded prizes by the former Maui Writers Conference, *Honolulu Magazine*, and the Southwest Writers Conference. The New York Public Library chose *Star-Crossed*, her young adult historical novel published by Alfred A. Knopf in 2006, to be among the *Books for the Teen Age —2007*. Linda and her husband, Bob Russell, have sailed many thousands of miles together aboard their own sailboat. Their time spent as voyage crewmembers on the HM Bark *Endeavour* inspired *Star-Crossed*, which has been republished for adult readers as *Barbados Bound*, followed by *Surgeon's Mate; Book Two of the Patricia MacPherson Nautical Adventure Series*.

Follow the author's blog and find reading guides at lindacollison.com.